Worm

"Everybody hates me... guess I'll go eat worms."

Cover Artwork by: Robert Ashley

Published by: CreateSpace Independent Publishing Platform

July 21, 2015

ISBN-10: 1515176193

ISBN-13: 978-1515176190

S.H.M.I.L.Y.

Thank you to those who pushed me to finally finish!

You know who you are!

Prologue: Palouse

"Andrews!" a burly man shouted over a walkie, frantically searching with his eyes around the warehouse.

A brunette crouched behind a wooden crate, covering her walkie with her knee, trying to silence the noise. Turning it off, she left it lay and crawled over to the other side. No one was in view and she had no idea where her partner was. Andrews pulled her gun from her belt, holding it outstretched as she stood. Shots fired from all directions. She crouched once again as she checked her body for wounds. Andrews knew she was no longer safe and had to either make a run for it or surrender herself to the drug dealers. Being twenty-four and in amazing athletic shape; the hotheaded detective stood, ignoring all gunshots and ran full speed toward the back wall. Earlier, she had seen a door leading to the outside over there and knew that was her only chance at escaping.

"Corey, I got her! She just ran to the loading docks," the man waved his pistol in the air. Holding the metal chains dangling from his neck as he ran, the unkempt man followed after Andrews.

Andrews had heard one of Corey's thugs calling and knew she would have to keep running. Looking behind her, she saw it was the youngest following her. Instead of going with the plan to keep running, she stopped suddenly and spun to face her attacker. She called out that she was a cop and when he didn't stop, she squeezed the trigger. The man instantly collapsed where he last stood. Andrews ran over, kicked the gun from his hand and stood over the body, her gun still aimed at him.

"You bitch!" Another guy came charging toward Andrews firing shots randomly. Corey was larger than his brother and the head dealer in this gang. Screaming as he ran, Corey was tackled by a burly man from the side, flipped to his stomach and then cuffed behind his back.

"You killed my little brother! I will get you for this lady; your head will be mine!" He spat at Andrews still flat on the ground.

Andrews laughed and walked over to where the man was being pinned. "Yes, and what a lovely head, I have, it's no wonder you want it. This was fun Corey; we should do it again sometime. As for your brother Johnny, I warned him, but he didn't stop. You have no one but yourself to blame for not teaching him to stop when someone says they're a cop." She shrugged her shoulders and started walking away from the scene.

After allowing another officer to take Corey, the burly man followed his partner, "You're an idiot Andrews. What the hell were you thinking back there? No, correction, you weren't thinking, you never do!"

Andrews turned to face the man, humor spread across her face. "Calm down Harrison, I'm fine. Do you see any blood, no! I knew what I was doing the entire time." She chuckled at his aggravated look and continued to walk out of the warehouse. "Corey has the worst aim, there was no real threat, and I really wasn't in danger."

"I still say you're an idiot. Plus, now you'll have a hit out on your head. I already have issues, protecting you; this isn't going to help at all. The chief won't like this, you do realize that, don't you?" Harrison, a man in his late thirties shook his head at the woman. He trusted her with his life and knew she would take a bullet for him, but, man did she give him a headache.

Still smiling to herself Andrews nodded her head, "No worries, my uncle will get over it. Uncle Pete or the chief rather" she rolled her eyes, "worries too much. He may try and get a hit on me, but with Corey in jail, I doubt anyone else would have the guts to kill off a police chief's niece."

Harrison grabbed his partner's shoulder and spun her to face him. "Your connections won't always protect you Bethany, eventually there will be someone who doesn't care if you're related to

Chief Mitchell or not. Just watch yourself, for my sake. It takes too long to get adjusted to a new partner."

Her smile faded as she saw how genuinely worried her partner really was. "Look, Jake, I'm sorry, okay? I know I take risks, but in my opinion, that's all part of the job. Getting the bad guys no matter what it takes. I will try and be smarter about my decisions from now on. Does that work for you?"

"Absolutely, even though I know you're full of it. Now let's get back to the station and do up the boat load of paperwork you just earned us with your shooting match." Harrison led Andrews out of the warehouse and to their car.

Back at the station they were congratulated by other detectives and officers for capturing two sons of a wanted drug lord, the only person that wasn't happy for them was Chief Mitchell. Andrews instantly knew she was in hot water when she saw her uncle's face and took note of him waving her into his office. Like the scolded child she was about to be, Andrews slowly made her way into his office and watched as her uncle closed the door and all the blinds behind her.

"Bethany, do you know what kind of trouble you just got yourself into? Already I have calls coming in from the undercover officers that there is a hit on your head. Do you know what my sister is going to do to me if she finds this out?" The chief sat at his desk and rested his head in his hands. "Couldn't you have been a normal girl and just played with dolls and clothes?"

"Uncle Pete I'm sorry, I did what I had to do and I did it by the book. What do you want me to do now? Go into hiding or witness protection?" Andrews knew that was a ridiculous suggestion and her uncle wouldn't dare send her off somewhere, but she honestly didn't know what he had expected her to say.

Sighing deeply, "Actually, that's what I am going to do with you. I have an old friend up in the Buffalo area and he owes me a favor. I'm sending you there until we can get this hit off your head."

"You can't be serious! What about Harrison? I have a life here! You can't just up and move me to another department! Buffalo! That's where people go when they want more snow, I hate the snow! What is mom going to think about this? You're being completely irrational Uncle Pete!" She started pacing around the room, rambling on about how unfair her uncle's decision was.

"Now Bee, the captain up there is doing me a favor so you need to be on your best behavior. Lay low for a little and try not to make a scene or get yourself in the news. No one knows about this except me and my buddy, so no one should be able to trace you. You cannot tell anyone about this, you got that? Not even your best friend, or your mother!" Chief Mitchell watched his niece as she began to grow pale in the face. They both knew keeping this from her mom was a mistake, but it had to be done.

The chief collected up papers on his desk and handed them to Andrews. "Take these and go straight home. Do not stop to talk to anyone, not even your partner. I will take care of the department here and make up some cover. I want you to pack up a few things and start driving to Buffalo, should take you about seven hours to get there. Once there I want you to go to this address, I already got you an apartment. All the information is on one of those papers. Your back story is there as well, memorize it and don't stray from what I wrote down." Taking her nodding as her, understanding he continued, "In the morning I want you to go to the station and talk to the captain first, no one else. He will give you an assignment and a partner for the time being. When things settle down here I will allow you to come back. I'm saving your life Bethany, please understand that." His heart broke watching his niece cry.

"No Uncle Pete, I get it and I appreciate what you're doing. I think it's a bit over the top, but I get it. I will do what you say, but only for a month, then I'm coming back, I refuse to be in Buffalo for the winter and it's already October. October is probably the start of their winter anyways, so I'm going to be miserable, I hope you realize that. I think I would rather get shot than have to play a cop in a blizzard. I loathe the snow." Wrinkling her nose, Andrews flipped through the papers she was just handed and grew overwhelmed by all the information she would need to memorize before the morning. She quickly wiped her eyes, hoping her uncle didn't see.

"Stay low Detective Andrews, and stay safe. Your mother would never forgive me if you died on the job so be smart about things and do not under any circumstances take risks!" The chief stood and gave his niece a hug before ushering her out the door. He watched as she walked out of the station, ignoring the pleas of her partner to stop. Just like that she was gone and he was left with the task of explaining her disappearance. It was definitely not something he was looking forward to.

Chapter 1: Earthworm

"Andrews! Woman, that's the third time today, you just took off without telling me! I'm your partner, there needs to be a sense of communication between us." An older but still strikingly handsome man shook his head at the woman crouched next to him.

Rolling her eyes, she smiled back, "Relax Baker, I know what I'm doing. This isn't my first time out in the field you know." Andrews crawled her way over to her partner and sat down next to him. She could see he was out of breath from running and then hiding. Geoff Baker had been assigned to her as a partner, she guessed the department thought someone near retirement would keep her calm and behind the desk. Assuming was a big mistake on their part, working behind a desk was definitely not something Andrews had any intention of doing.

The man just looked at his partner. He couldn't help but like her even with the craziness. She probably added to his receding hairline though. The gray had been there before, well maybe she helped add to the gray in his mustache and beard, but he had been gray on his way to white long before she showed up. It was an interesting situation though, and he thought back to that first day he met her when the captain just called him into the office and told him he was getting a new partner and not to ask any questions but to keep her safe. Geoff remembered how he thought she would get him killed and, not surprisingly, he was still thinking that same thought. Andrews hasn't slowed down since she got to the department and he wasn't as young as he used to be. Keeping up with the spit-fire was difficult, especially since taking orders didn't seem to be something she knew how to do.

"So Baker, you ready to take them down? Cover me and I'll go in through the left." She saw the questioning look coming back at her suggestion and instead of waiting for him to disagree, she counted it down. "Ready? One, two... go!"

Andrews sprinted from around the crate and charged toward the other side of the wall, making sure to duck between the shelves and weave her way there to avoid being hit by the rapid gunfire. She knew her partner would cover her, she trusted him now, and so she gave up worrying about getting shot a long time ago. Holding her gun out in front of her, she aimed at the men standing in her view and fired at their legs. All hits. The men fell to the ground and Andrews could hear Baker running his way to her. Rolling each of the men on the ground over, the detectives cuffed them and read them their Miranda rights.

Baker just shook his head, "you're going to give me a heart attack one of these days girly. They were just a couple of art smugglers, but yet you had to go charging in, guns blazing like we were at a good ol' fashioned Western shootout."

"Wasn't worth the risk of letting them get away, charging was the logical approach." Andrews knew that really it wasn't, but to her it was the best way to go about the job. Kept things interesting, plus, getting shot as always, helped raise the adrenaline levels. Technically, she could be labeled an adrenaline junkie and in her mind, there was nothing wrong with that fact.

"They weren't going to get away, they were almost out of ammo, weren't you counting?" Geoff reached for his walkie and called it in. Back up had been waiting outside of the warehouse so it wasn't long before other officers walked in and took the smugglers away.

Baker led the way to his car with Andrews tailing behind him. They had their own ritual for after a case was closed, going to Bill Gray's for a world's famous cheeseburger and loganberry drink. It was a little out of the way, but they had made a friend in the college boy Robert that ran the place at night. He enjoyed hearing about their daily activities and they reveled in the feeling of being young once more. Reaching the joint, they both ordered their usual and had a quick conversation with Rob and then went to sit at *their* booth. They had claimed a specific booth and even left a sign on the table for those who tried to sit there would know it was reserved by the Buffalo detective unit.

"You realize you've been here four months today Bee?" Geoff watched her face go a little pale and then almost as quickly as the color had gone it flooded back and her smile returned.

Bee nodded and thought carefully before making a comment back. "Yeah, kind of crazy to believe, huh? I actually wasn't expecting to hang around this long, but it seems like I may never leave now."

The call had come a month ago that the hit was still out there, but Corey's goons weren't able to figure out that she had left the state. For now she was still safe, but it felt like she would never get to return home. It had been four months of no contact with friends or family from back home; to her it was like they didn't exist anymore. Bethany had completely rebuilt her life and started fresh, this was becoming home to her now, which was not a feeling she enjoyed.

"You want to talk about it?" It hadn't taken him long to figure out that there was more to her moving to Buffalo than the captain or Bethany had let on. He knew there was something big that they weren't telling him, but he couldn't even begin to figure out what. Geoff had just been told to keep her safe and out of the press, the latter being a harder task than one would think. The girl had a way of causing a scene and making things a tad more dramatic than they should be.

"There's nothing to talk about. I'll just be happy when it finally stops snowing."

His chuckle sounded more like a roar because of his bass voice, "Yes, I believe everyone knows how much you hate the snow. That is something you have made quite clear Bethany. So, what are your plans for the night?"

Bethany knew she didn't have a family to go home to like he did; she didn't really have any friends she could call up and go to a movie or out to a club. She hated sounding pathetic though, so as cheery as possible she always tried to convince him she would be fine on her own and he didn't need to invite her over. Sure, his wife, Valerie loved having her over and talking about their daughter's wedding, coming up, but she always felt like she was intruding on their family and didn't feel like letting him guilt her into it tonight. "Actually, I have plans with my friend Ben. I think we're going to meet up with one of his coworkers Jerry for some ice cream later." Ok, so it was a sad excuse and attempt, but it was true, she really was going to meet up with Ben and Jerry for ice cream, just they weren't people. There was a new flavor that was just released that she wanted to try out.

"Uh huh, well you have fun with Ben and Jerry. You let them know that Perry and Hershey say hi for me." He may be old but he wasn't slow. He knew exactly what she meant. He had caught her numerous times eating a pint of ice cream while doing paperwork back at the station. It was her way of coping and it was a better way than most come up with.

Finishing their meals, they both got in the car and Geoff drove his partner back to the station. He dropped her off near the front of her car and headed home to his wife and three daughters. A house full of estrogen was just the thing he looked forward to after a long day at work. Andrews walked into the station before heading to her car; she had forgotten a folder on her desk she wanted to do some research tonight. When she got to her desk, though there was an envelope with her name on it. Opening the letter, she gasped as she read what the note said; *I found you, and now I'm going to kill you.*

Pulling herself together, Andrews headed toward the captain's office and knocked on the door before entering. He lifted his head and gave her a questioning glance. She hadn't been to see him since she first got there, Captain Harris just figured she blamed him for her being there longer than a month and excused her behavior. Holding out the letter she took a seat across from him and watched as his face grew stern. Without saying anything to her, he picked up the phone and asked his secretary to patch him through to the chief of the Colebrookdale Police back in Boyertown.

"Is this the first letter you've gotten Andrews?" Captain Harris assumed she would have come to him sooner if there was something else but figured it was safer to ask. Andrews seemed to be the type to handle things on her own first before asking for help, she was a determined independent woman, the very thing that caused her to end up on his detective team.

She glanced up from her lap and nodded, "Yes sir, this was the first I heard of anything having to do with my case back home."

"Have you talked to anyone else about this?" He raised his eyebrows trying to read her face.

"No, sir, I saw the envelope on my desk, opened it and then came directly to your office."

Captain Harris raised a finger to silence her as he began talking into the phone to her real chief. "Yeah, this was the first one she got, is the guy still in jail?" He paused, "I can keep her tied to her desk till we figure this out, and that shouldn't be a problem. It's slow here." Jeff Harris noticed the look on the young detective's face as he mentioned giving her busy work, he knew she would hate every minute of that but this was about her safety not her being bored. "Don't worry about it, I promised you I'd keep her alive and I plan on keeping that promise. Geoff has grown attached to her too, actually the whole department has." Laughing, he closed up the conversation, "Oh I know I have to give her back. Alright, will do. Keep me posted."

"Well? You're going to stick me on desk duty till you catch this guy, is that it? You know that isn't going to work, right? Didn't chief tell you that won't work?" Bethany was growing frustrated at everyone trying to control her life and make decisions for her. She still would have liked taking the chance on her head and just stayed back in Boyertown.

He rubbed his forehead, "He told me you wouldn't go for that, so here's the deal. Right now there are no more cases for you and Geoff; I was going to have you both work on some old cases

14

anyways. You will stick with that until something comes up and if I run out of detective teams and you guys are the only ones left, then fine, you can take the case but for now you are on desk duty until further notice. Do not disobey that, I promised to keep you alive and damn it Bethany I will do that even if I have to cuff you to your desk myself or put you in a holding cell. Understand?"

"Yes, sir. Can you at least keep me posted on the letter though, and what's going on with Corey?" She understood why the chief and captain were doing this, but she didn't like it one bit and she had every intention of looking into it herself.

"I will keep you informed with information you need to know. Also, I want you to keep this, between us and not tell Baker yet. If things get worse, we'll let him in but for now I think it's best that only the three of us know what's going on."

"Fine."

A month passed with no big cases or breaks in her own case. Andrews was getting bored of doing research and felt useless even though they had put to rest two of the old cases they had been working on. It was time to get back out into the field and luckily for Andrews her wish was answered. All other detectives were busy on their own cases so when the call came in about a woman found strangled, the only ones left to take the case were Baker and Andrews.

Geoff had taken the call and grabbed the keys from his desk, "Come on Andrews, looks like we have ourselves a dead twenty-something. She was strangled with a true ribbon and left on the sidewalk down by Franklin and Mohawk. Some homeless man called it in."

Following her partner out to the car, Andrews hoped she didn't look too excited at the news of a young woman being strangled. For goodness sake's the girl was almost her age, technically that could be her out there all cold and lifeless. "I'm sorry the girl is dead, but it's good to get out from behind the desk, finally. I was starting to think Batman was protecting the city with few homicides there were."

"I don't think it's the fact that crime went down, I think it was more of the captain assigning everyone but cases. You wouldn't know why that is would you? I had asked him, but he didn't really give me a reason, he just avoided answering my question each time." Geoff knew his partner had the scoop but he didn't want to push her. She would tell him when she was ready and until then he would trust her and the captain.

Andrews shook her head in exasperation, "I don't know Geoff, I tried to get us a case a few times, but he kept telling me no." It wasn't the total truth but she had argued with the captain a few times to give them a case, even just a smaller one.

Upon arriving at the scene, they realized they weren't the first ones to get there. The medical examiner's van was already there and Norman Vance the local M.E. was already probing the body. Andrews thought he was an extremely bizarre man, but she figured he would have to be in order to work with the dead all day long. He was brilliant though, and knew his stuff better than the M.E. had back home. Then again, he was Geoff's age and nearing sixty fast, he held lots of years of experience.

"Hey Norm, what do we have?" Baker crouched next to his friend and waited for the extensive description of the woman he was about to receive. He always gives more information than he cared to know, but it was hard to train the old dog to give less. It just became easier to hear the entire speech and just take from it what he needed to know.

Norm looked up from the body while he extracted the probe from the girl's liver. "Well, she's been dead about twelve hours. I won't know for sure till I get her back to the morgue, but from the tree ribbon around her neck and the bruising I'd say she died from strangulation. She looks to be about mid-twenties." He picked up her hand and set it back down and then looked over the rest of her slowly. "She was right handed, wore contacts and looks to be as though she was a swimmer."

Geoff shook his head, "Alright, Norm I'm going to stop you there. Go through her pockets and let me know if there's an id."

The medical examiner searched through the woman's sweatshirt pockets and pulled out a school ID card. He handed it over to Baker and stood up. Andrews moved in with the camera and began documenting the scene. She took note of the workout clothes the victim was wearing, nothing was ripped or torn. Her clothes were still zipped and seemed to be in perfect order. There was no sign of struggle; any scratch marks or blood. The only sign of trouble was the bruising around the girl's neck. Things were too nice and neat that it made things seem posed.

"Baker, does she look like she was placed here and arranged into the pose? Anyone that's strangled would have fought back and then collapsed in some sort of screwy way. They wouldn't look like they had just laid down to take a nap." Andrews continued snapping pictures of the girl and her surroundings.

Her partner crouched down and leaned to peer under where the girl lay. "I see what you mean. There's no sign of her being dragged either, the dirt isn't disturbed under her. Her name is Leah Kummer by the way, at least that's whose card was on her." He glanced up from the card and noticed her one hand was tightly clenched and there seemed to be something moving inside.

Andrews caught her partner's attention freezing on the girl's hand. She pulled out a pen and handed it to Baker. Watching as he poked at the hand and opened it, she jumped as something wriggled its way out. She quickly stepped back as to not step on it and started to laugh at her ridiculousness of the situation.

Baker still had a quizzical look on his face. "A worm? Seriously. She was holding an earthworm?" He scratched his head with the back of his hand, "Is that her pet worm? Why would a college student be carrying around a worm?"

"I feel like that should be a trick question Geoff. I honestly have no idea why anyone would be carrying around a worm. I don't even think Frank would do that, and he's a forensic entomologist." Andrews leaned down and took pictures of the worm trying to wiggle away.

Norm held up his finger, "If I may suggest, bag up our slimy little friend and take it back to Frank. He might be able to tell where the worm had started its travels before bumping into our girl here. Dirt has its own type of fingerprinting, could be helpful."

"Andrews let's get back to the station and start doing some of the background. Norm, give me a call when you're done with the vic please." Geoff waved over an officer and instructed him to bag the worm, getting that to the entomologist; and to get the pictures developed and on his desk in two hours.

Walking back to the car, Andrews stopped before opening the door and caught her partner's glance. Nodding her head back, she questioned him, "You see that guy standing by the lamppost? The one in uniform, who is that?"

Baker tried to be slick as he leaned so he could see past her and looked over the officer she had pointed out. Not knowing who that was he just shrugged his shoulders, hoping she would clue him in as to why she was asking. She couldn't really expect him to know everyone's name in the department. Buffalo was a larger city and well, there was a lot of crime. There were more officers at the rookie level than people who didn't eat Buffalo wings. Knowing all their names was impossible.

"I was just asking because I haven't seen him before. I thought I knew all the officers by now, but he doesn't look familiar. That's all, wasn't super important." Andrews knew it would bother her until she found out his name. It made her feel less like an outcast knowing who people were and having a little background on them. That way, when she passed them at the station, she could ask about their families instead of just nodding in their direction and grunting like she was some sort of primitive Neanderthal.

Of course she would know everyone why did that even surprise him? "Whatever Andrews, just get in the car so we can go", he opened his own door and got in, shutting the door behind him.

The battle over the radio always frustrated the detectives. Baker enjoyed the classics, listening to the hits of the decades and reminiscing about his youthful days. Andrews, on the other hand, wanted to stay current and always changed the classic rock to the hits of today's youth. Eventually they both gave in and just shut the radio off, fuming at how stubborn the other was.

"So Bethany, tell me about your family. You never really ever mentioned, if you have any siblings, or where your parents are. I'm guessing you don't have a boyfriend since you pretty much live at the station or in your apartment. I don't even know where you grew up. All I know is you're not from Buffalo." Geoff glanced over and watched as she grew ridged and looked out the window.

Bethany closed her eyes, it was only a matter of time he would ask her this. It was possible though to tell him about her and not put herself in danger. "Well, I was born in a small town in Pennsylvania where my parents still live. I have a younger brother. Once upon a time I was engaged, but obviously that didn't work out. That's pretty much it." She hoped he'd drop it, but knew he was oblivious to her feelings and how to properly react to them.

"You were engaged? Did you break it off or did he? I don't know why anyone would let you go, you're such a catch. The whole annoying got to be independent attitude and all, such a sought after trait in women." The sarcasm just seeped from his words.

She snickered at his comment, "Actually, I kind of just took off and didn't tell him I was leaving. Guess you could say I broke it off."

Geoff stopped at a red traffic light and turned his entire body toward Bethany, "You did what?"

"Oh, I just took off. I didn't tell anyone I was leaving; I just got in the car and drove to Buffalo. Haven't talked to anyone since." She shrugged acting as though it were no big deal, like it was normal for people to just take off without a word.

"Well, alright then."

The pair arrived back at the station and was greeted by a frantic young officer. "Detective Andrews, the captain has been looking for you everywhere. He isn't very happy he hasn't found you either. He would like to see you in his office now."

"Right, this can't be good. Geoff get started, I'll make up the board when I get back. Your handwriting is atrocious, so please just don't even try and do it yourself." She smiled at him to let him know things were okay and they would discuss whatever it was later.

Walking to Captain Harris' office, she wondered if another note had showed up. Maybe this was good news, and she could go home now. Entering through the door her heart immediately fell when she recognized the man sitting across from the captain. "Oh, this can't be good", she regretted everything she had ever done all in that one moment.

"I see you know our visitor, Detective. Please, have a seat." Captain Harris waved his head directing Andrews toward an empty chair next to the man.

The visitor held out his hand to Andrews, "Nice to see you again Detective."

"You too, Topher. Didn't have any other detectives to harass back home, you had to come all the way out to Buffalo?" Andrews had a thing about lawyers. In her opinion majority of them were scum and only thought of themselves. This man was the king of those lawyers; he ruled over them and destroyed anyone that got in his path. She had come up against Christopher Rollins multiple times over cases and now he was here in her city, probably ready to throw her under the bus again.

Captain Harris folded his hands and rested his head upon them, "Andrews be nice to our guest, he came here to offer you a way out of the mess you're in."

Skeptical of the last statement given by the captain, Andrews turned to the lawyer waiting for this "way out" as it was called. "Go ahead Topher, fix everything for me", she sneered raising her eyebrows at the slime sitting before her. He had a motive, she knew he did, it was just a matter of time till it became known.

"I want you to testify that you were wrong to shoot Johnny, and…" Topher didn't get to finish. The well-dressed man with slicked back hair and watched as he got verbally attacked.

"You want me to what!" Andrews knew it had to be bad, but testify that what she did was wrong? There was no way she would ever do that! She wasn't wrong to shoot his sorry ass, he deserved it. He was the one chasing her with a gun and threatening her, it was all in self-defense.

"AND, I want you to come out of hiding so we can catch whoever was connected with the crime. Corey is still behind bars and we would like this case to become closed. We think it's in the state's best interest if you offer yourself as bait." Preparing for her to lash out at him, he squinted his eyes.

Andrews calmed herself down, bait. They wanted her to be bait and to lure the criminals out of hiding so they could have a shot at killing her, all to close the case because apparently the detectives back home couldn't do their job. "You can't be serious. You want me to risk my life because you guys can't do what you're paid to do and catch the bad guys."

The captain sat silent, watching the exchange between the two. He had thought it was a ridiculous notion himself, but he had to let Andrews have a chance to decline it herself before he put a stop to the nonsense. "Alright counselor that's enough. Detective Andrews has declined your offer so you may take that back to whomever and please just inform us when there is no longer a hit on the detective. Thank you for coming, and don't hesitate to stop by at any time to give us an update of your progress."

The lawyer took the hint, thanking the captain and excusing himself from the room. "Bethany, I just want you to know that they sooner this is all over the sooner you can come home. Your family thinks you're dead. Kevin hired a private investigator to find you and when he came up with nothing they held a memorial service for you. You need to go home and fix this, one way or another."

She was in shock. Andrews realized that rumors would spread about her disappearance but she couldn't believe they all thought she was dead. It had only been a few months, why hadn't the chief clued them in at least a little. "Captain, what am I supposed to do? Would offering myself as bait be the right choice here?"

"I honestly don't know what you should do. For now stick to the plan and we'll take it a day at the time. Go back and help Baker on our current case and continue to keep a low profile." He felt for her, he really did. Captain Harris couldn't imagine how it must feel to know everyone that means something thinks you're dead. Poor girl.

"Alright." Andrews got up and left his office. She stood for a minute outside the door and tried to collect herself. Whether it was a gift or a curse, she had the ability to just shove emotion to the side and become cold. Now it was a gift and she was extremely thankful for it as she walked back to her desk and put on an act so Baker wouldn't catch on.

Geoff glanced up from his computer, "Ah, Miss Popular returns. And just what were you summoned for this time, your highness? Bully any rookies lately? Break another rule?"

"C, all of the above", she laughed. "Nah, he just wanted to have a chat with me. Nothing serious. So what have you been up to since I was in there? Nothing it looks like, way to leave all the work for me! Jerk."

"Hey now! I did a lot; give me a little more credit. I may be twice your age, but I know my way around a computer and here is the background on our little worm girl." He handed his partner a folder containing the information he had found on Leah Kummer.

Andrews walked over to the white board and picked up a marker. Making sure to get all the spellings right, she put the information up on the board, leaving room for what they were still missing. "Alright, so it looks like we already have a few people we can talk to, let's start with her roommate." She picked up a different marker and circled the name, Frankie Gerald in blue.

"Want to take bets on if that's a male or female?" He grabbed the keys from his desk and stood.

She smiled, "I say it's a girl and the wager is the loser has to pay for coffee for the next week."

"Deal."

A short time later they had arrived at the University at Buffalo's north campus. The victim had lived in a double apartment right on campus in Creekside village. Geoff laughed when they drove up to the building and it sunk in that the roommate would have to be female since it was a school apartment. Looked like he'd be buying the coffee all next week.

Knocking on apartment 3B, Andrews puts her ear to the door and tried to listen for any noise coming from inside. Hearing nothing, she tried the handle and found it unlocked. Procedure would say not to go in but being a stickler for breaking as many procedural rules as possible, Andrews let herself in announcing that she was with the Buffalo police. Again hearing nothing, she motioned for Baker to follow her, both detectives holding their pistols now down by their sides. The apartment was in complete disarray, more than what was normal for college. They made their way through the different rooms and then saw the one bedroom door was already ajar.

"You first." Andrews nodded toward Baker.

Snickering, "Gee, thanks. Send the old man first, get him shot and out of the way."

Andrews rolled her eyes, "Fine you big baby, I'll go." She held her gun out in front of her and kicked the door opening, aiming into the room. She suddenly froze when she realized there was a leg sticking out from behind the bed. First checking to make sure nothing was behind the door she rushed over to the body and saw it was a woman and she was lying in a pool of blood.

"Looks like you found Frankie. Don't touch anything, I'll call it in." Geoff left the room and pulled out his phone to call in the crime techs, and Norm.

She watched for her partner to reenter the room before motioning him over to her side. "Look, there's something moving in her hand too. What do you want to bet it's another earthworm?"

"Double or nothing on the coffee bet." Geoff raised his eyebrows daring his partner.

"We're sick, you know that. No wonder the captain makes us get psych evaluations every week." Andrews loved those; it was entertaining for her and Baker to mess with the shrink's mind.

Thinking the same thing as his partner he just laughed at her comment, "We're not sick, this is just how we cope with the mess known as murder. It's what keeps us sane."

Inspecting the rest of the apartment until everyone else showed up, the detectives found nothing more of interest. Finally Norm arrived and they both pointed toward the back room, following the medical examiner as he led them in there. Norm sighed heavily as he saw the young woman's body and shook his head. This part of the job never became easier for him.

"I haven't finished the first girl and now you find me another. Considering you were here first, you must know who she is." Norm looked up from the probe he had just pulled, marking down the temperature of the woman's liver on his sheet.

"It's the roommate, Frankie. We were coming to question her and found the door unlocked, the place in shambles and this girl dead behind the bed." Baker rushed through the explanation. He was interested to see what was in the girl's hand, he'd admit that was the only reason he was still hanging around.

Norm shook his head again, "Such a shame. Ah and look here, it appears you have another wriggling friend in this girl's hand. I believe that is your connection between the murders, certainly one I've never seen before."

More officers arrived on the scene and soon the place was overly crowded. "Andrews let's just continue with our list of people to question, let them clean this up. I don't want to take the chance of getting behind whoever is doing this and happening upon another victim."

Andrews agreed with her partner, she really wanted to just find someone to talk to so maybe they could start finding answers instead of creating more questions. Out of the corner of her eye, she spotted that same detective again and decided now was an awful time but she was going to introduce herself anyways. She left her partners side and made her way across the room to the unknown officer.

"Hi, I'm Bethany Andrews, I don't believe we met before", she offered up her hand.

Accepting the introduction, the officer smiled back at the detective. "Hi yourself, I'm Junior. We have met before, you sent me on a coffee run a few weeks ago. It's ok that you don't remember though, I'm just a rookie. I know where I stand on the food chain around here."

Attitude, nice. "Right, well sorry about that. Have a good day then." She smiled at him and excused herself going back over to her partner. "Snippy little devil."

"Haha, well what did you expect Andrews?" Geoff was constantly being amused by his partner's antics. Entertained him throughout the day at least.

They left and Andrews missed the younger officer watching her till she disappeared from his sight. Getting back in the car, Andrews checked the folder and pulled another address with a name. It was the first victim's parents. They lived close to the campus in Clarence so it should be a quick drive. Reading the profile on each parent she just had to laugh at how distinguished they both were. The girl's mother was a children's author and professor in the classics department at Buffalo State College, and then the father was a congressman for the state senator. This visit was going to be a blast, she could already tell.

The car ride was silent and Geoff didn't even put up a fight when Andrews changed the station to what he would call screaming, not music. Pulling up to the house though he finally spoke, "Great, they're rich."

"Uh, is that a tennis court in the back yard? You have got to be kidding me. Then again, he works for the senator and she's an author and a professor. Guess it makes sense. Let's just go get this over with." Andrews unbuckled and let herself out of the car. She followed her partner up to the front door where they were greeted by a maid and a barking little white ball of fur.

Geoff looked down at the dog and then back up at the maid, "Mr. and Mrs. Kummer please?"

The maid bowed to the detectives, shutting the door on them again. "Does that mean they aren't home?" Andrews questioned.

"Who the heck knows, all I know is that thing does not deserve to be called a dog that was a rat covered in lint."

Still laughing at her partners comment as the door opened again, Andrews did her best to keep a straight face. Before them stood a man dressed in a suit with a woman clinging to his arm in a fancy lounge wear getup. She took a guess that the news of their daughter wasn't going to surprise them at all, the whole thing already felt scripted and fake.

"Mr. and Mrs. Kummer, we're from the Buffalo police department. We have some unfortunate news about your daughter Leah. May we please come in?" Baker made a move to walk through the door, forcing the couple to back up and let the detectives in.

Andrews took in the foyer as these people probably called it. It honestly looked bigger than her entire apartment. This house could eat her house back home and still be hungry. She couldn't understand why people felt the need to have so much room, and she would really hate having to clean this place. Then again, that's what the maid was for.

They were led into a sitting room that looked like it was made up to receive a queen. The detectives just looked at each other kind of scared to sit on the couch for fear of ruining the upholstery. "You have a lovely home." Andrews thought playing the polite card would be a good idea in this case.

"Why thank you dear. You said you had information about our daughter. Has something happened to her?" Mrs. Kummer reached over and put her hand on her husband's. There was no sign of worry or curiosity on her face. There really wasn't a sign of any emotion; her face didn't seem to allow such a thing.

Watching the reactions closely Baker broke the news, "I'm very sorry to tell you but your daughter was found murdered this morning."

Nothing. No gasp, no screams, no tears, there was absolutely nothing coming from either of the Kummers. Were these people robots, or was there just too much Botox that they couldn't show emotion. Did they not care or did they already know? Andrews was very confused. She had hoped this wasn't how her parents reacted when the private investigator came back and told them and Kevin that he couldn't find anything on her.

"Yes, to be honest detectives," Mr. Kummer paused as he looked at his wife, "that news does not really surprise us." The graying man pushed his glasses up before continuing. "Our daughter was a free spirit of sorts. She despised our way of life and was into things we never approved of. She liked to do whatever she could to upset her mother and me. It was only a matter of time things caught up to her."

Mrs. Kummer leaned forward, "Don't get us wrong detectives, we absolutely loved our daughter. We tried to get her help numerous of times but she simply wouldn't hear of it. She didn't think she was doing anything wrong and there's only so much you can do for a person that doesn't accept your assistance."

"Ma'am, when was the last time you had heard from your daughter?" Baker wished he was surprised by their response but he really wasn't. This was just how it was in the city with the "superior" folk as they saw themselves.

The couple again looked at each other. "It would have to have been last week; she called to let us know that she was sending our check back. She didn't want our financial help to pay for college. Her and her father got into a fight and we hadn't heard from her since."

Andrews turned her gaze to Mr. Kummer, "Did she mention anything else to you about school, or her roommate perhaps?"

"Leah never talked about school or her friends. We don't even know any of their names. She made sure to keep us out of the loop with anything like that." Mr. Kummer let go of his wife's hand and stood. "Would either of you like a drink?"

The detectives declined the offer, and Mr. Kummer walked out of the room leaving his wife alone. She sat up straighter as she asked the detectives, "How did it happen? Can you tell me if she suffered at all?"

Geoff looked down at his shoes and then at Mrs. Kummer, "Ma'am your daughter was strangled. That's all we know as of now. We are working hard on the case though and will do our best to find who did this to her."

"I would actually prefer not to know if you don't mind. She cut us out of her life and now that she's gone I would rather just keep her out of my life if that is alright by you. It was hard enough to watch her throw her life away. I don't think I could handle knowing what kind of trouble got her murdered." The woman twisted her wedding ring around her finger and kept her eyes low, unable to look at the detectives for fear of being judged.

Andrews glanced at her partner and then stood up walking over to the fireplace and taking note of the pictures on the mantel. Baker followed suit and when Mr. Kummer came back into the room they thanked the couple for letting them in. Handing them his business card, Baker asked the Kummers to call him if they thought of anything that may help, had questions or were contacted by anyone else.

After they left Andrews turned to her partner, "Geoff there's a problem."

"You mean other than the fact they don't even care their daughter was murdered?" Geoff shook his head at the whole situation.

"Yeah, the man in the picture with Leah, I know him." Andrews felt her body going cold in a mix of fear and confusion.

Geoff questioned his partner's mental stability, she looked like she was about to have a breakdown. "How do you know him? I didn't recognize him and I know everyone you know."

Andrews looked up at her partner, tears forming in her eyes, "Geoff, that's my fiancé. That was Kevin in that picture."

Chapter 2: Dew-Worm

"What do you mean that was Kevin?" Geoff looked at his partner completely in shock that not only had her past been brought up but that it was uncovered because of the case.

Bethany sighed and closed her eyes for a moment, "We'll talk about it tomorrow. I need time to think."

"Alright, take your time. Why don't I take you back to the station to get your car and then you can go home for the rest of the day. I will take care of scheduling interviews and getting everything ready. "He glanced at her from time to time while driving, worry creased his forehead. " I want to call Leah's parents back in for some more questions. "

She just nodded and stared out the window. The car was once again filled with an uncomfortable silence. So many questions passed through her mind and she couldn't believe Kevin hadn't told her he had family up in Buffalo. Uncle Pete would have never sent her here if that were the case, now there was the possibility of running into him. That was something that couldn't happen. Arriving at the station, she got in her car and drove home.

The next morning Andrews didn't feel like getting out of bed and for the first time in her entire career being on the force, she called in sick. Since the captain didn't even argue with her, she assumed Geoff had filled him in and knew she was in for a lecture when she got back. She spent the day lounging around the house, not thinking about anything in particular and just doing chores in a robotic state. Looking at the clock later in the day, she realized how much time had already passed and that it was nearing seven already. Geoff had left a message that he scheduled the interviews for ten am on Thursday morning, tomorrow. Andrews checked her calendar and shook her head at how it was already March 2011 and she was still in Buffalo. Rather than staying up longer, she decided it was probably best to get to bed early and wake up refreshed. Hopefully the extra sleep would help her out.

Arriving at the station a little before ten, Andrews met her partner by his desk and followed him into one of the interrogation rooms. The Kummers were already in there and Geoff took lead, sitting down opposite them at the only piece of furniture in the room, a small wooden table. He passed back a folder to Andrews making sure to tape on a sticky note directly on top of the file. She read it to herself and noted Geoff's instructions to her to keep her cool and let him run this one alone. Apparently Geoff thought she'd lose it and start asking about Kevin. She may have a lot of questions but she knew how to be professional about the situation.

"Thank you for coming in Mr. and Mrs. Kummer. I realized we just talked a couple of days ago but we just wanted to follow up with some more questions and make sure we got straight what we had questioned about before." Geoff took the file back from his partner and opened it, flipping through some papers. It was all an act but it was an important one when conducting an interrogation.

Mr. Kummer sat up straighter and folded his hands on the table. "It was our pleasure, anything to help you find who did this to our daughter."

Baker just nodded at the man who clearly hadn't gained any emotion since when they had told him his daughter was found murdered. Being a father himself he couldn't even imagine not caring about his baby girl being taken from him in this manner. "You said before you didn't really know much about Leah's friends at all. Is that correct?"

"Yes, that is correct. She kept her life to herself and we were in the dark about everything." Mr. Kummer held a stern, steady voice and got straight to the point with his answer.

"You never heard mention of Frankie, nor had the girl over for a party? You didn't know anything about the girl?" Baker looked up from the papers in front of him and watched the man's expression. Nothing changed; he simply just nodded at the questions.

Andrews was holding her tongue as best as she could but these people were starting to agitate her and she really couldn't hold it in much longer. She knew Geoff would probably kick her out of the room for this but she just had to know. The man she had planned on marrying kept these people from her and she was starting to see that maybe that was for the best, but she just had to know why. Moving out of the shadows she stood in front of the table and looked down at the people she might have had to call family.

"Tell me about your nephew Kevin. Was he close to Leah? Do you know where he is? Might he know more about her life than you do?" Andrews caught the glare from her partner and ignored it and kept eye contact with the Kummers.

Mrs. Kummer looked up this time and a look of sadness crossed her eyes, "He's my sister's boy. He grew up with Leah and she was like a sister to him. I know they talked a lot but a few months ago Kevin seemed to just disappear, he has been searching for someone and my sister only hears from him once a month anymore. She said he's in turmoil over some girl running away and he can't seem to let go." She looked down at her hands, "If you do happen to find him though, please let me know so I can tell my sister he's doing ok."

That was the end of keeping her cool. Andrews felt the tears welding up in her eyes and knew she had crossed a line. Excusing herself she quickly exited the room so the Kummers wouldn't see her cry. Outside the door she leaned against the wall and tried to collect herself. Geoff came out a little later and just stood there watching her.

"I told you to stay quiet. I told you not to ask about Kevin. I told you I would run this one." He saw how upset she was and decided not to yell at her anymore, they could discuss it later when she had calmed down. "I'm going to be bringing them out now, either make yourself sparse or pull it together for a moment.

"I'll be okay, you can bring them out." She wiped a tear from her eye and took a couple of deep breaths. "I'm okay", she said more for trying to convince herself than Geoff.

He felt kind of bad for the girl, to find out something like this about her fiancé was rather a harsh reality. Baker walked back into the interrogation room and ushered out the Kummers, thanking them for their cooperation and leading them down the hall. A few minutes later he returned and found Andrews still standing in the same spot he had left her. He just opened the door to the room back up and pointed for her to go in. She complied, it was quite the snail pace but she moved. Pulling the one chair out he motioned for her to take a seat and then went and sat opposite her himself.

"You're either going to explain everything to me right now or I'm going to the captain and telling him you're emotionally attached to the case and he should find someone else to work it." His eyes were stern but open; he really wanted her to just tell him what was going on and stop keeping secrets.

Anger flashed through Bethany's eyes. She was not emotionally attached to the case. Yes the first victim happened to be the cousin of her ex- fiancé but that ex part in front of the title must mean something. It had been months since she had seen or spoken to Kevin, and sure Mrs. Kummer said he was out looking for a girl but that didn't mean it was her. "Geoff, I am okay and go ahead and tell the captain, see where that gets you."

Geoff knew that tone, he had been partners with this girl long enough to know she was daring him. There really was more to this whole thing than he knew and later he would deal with it but there were more people coming in about the case. Thankfully it wasn't anyone else connected to the Leah side of the case really. "Frankie's boyfriend should be here soon. Think you can make it through the interrogation without breaking down again?"

"I'm fine, Geoff. I know how to do my job, just please stop treating me like I'm fragile and going to break." She was frustrated by his babying her but knew it was genuine concern for her. They were partners and he cared about her wellbeing, plus he had always been like a father figure since day one, not that it bothered her since she had no idea where her dad was or if he was even alive.

To save her from having to talk anymore to Geoff about the situation his phone rang. He answered, told her to stay put and then left the room. A moment or so later he came back with an attractive man who looked to be in his early twenties. He looked like one of those guys that beat to his own drum. He had a goatee and was dressed in a casual and yet artsy style. Andrews stood to let Geoff sit down in her place but he motioned for her to stay seated and handed her the file. Again there was a note on the cover but this time it was encouragement that she could handle this and to take it easy.

"Mr. Banner, what was your relationship with the victim Frankie Gerald?" She had already seen in the file what his relationship was but it was always better to get them to admit it out loud for themselves.

The man tipped his hat down over his forehead a little and leaned back in the chair. "She was my soul mate, the ying to my yang."

Andrews closed her eyes and tried not to chuckle at the man's response. "So you were dating then, correct?"

"Yes we were together, we were intimate too if you need to know that." His coolness was coming across as being ignorant.

"Okay, Mr. Banner-"

"Jason. Call me Jason", he interrupted.

She nodded, "Okay Jason, when was the last time you saw Ms. Gerald?" Andrews drew out a pen from her pocket and scribbled a little note on the folder and held it so Geoff could see over her shoulder. She was starting to think this kid was on something, or high or just really weird. Andrews figured asking Geoff would be smart; he could keep an eye on him while she continued to question the man. If he agreed, well then at least they had a reason to lock him up if that was necessary.

Jason squinted his eyes in thought, "I think it was a few days ago. She told me she had a few exams coming up and that she would be crazy busy. I told her that was fine; there was a festival I wanted to attend anyways."

"How did she seem when you talked to her? Was she happy, sad, worried, or angry about anything? Andrew jotted down what the man was telling her making sure to denote the man's attitude while answering.

"She seemed at peace with everything. She wasn't anxious or seeming to be upset for any reason if that's what you mean. Just told me she had to study and that her and her roommate was going to go out that night so I shouldn't bother going over." He leaned on the table and held his head up with his hand.

Pausing, Andrews watched how relaxed the man in front of her was considering his soul mate was dead. Or was it that he didn't know what had happened to Frankie? "Jason, do you know where Ms. Gerald is right now?"

His eyes widened and he smirked, "Well detective, considering you called me in here; she's probably in this building somewhere. Either in jail or down in the morgue. So which one is it?"

"Sir, I'm very sorry to have to be the one to tell you this but we found your girlfriend at her residence a few days ago. She had been murdered." For a moment Andrews thought she saw disappointment flash across his face and through for sure he was going to grieve over the news. Instead he remained cool and collected.

"Somehow that doesn't surprise me. That roommate of hers was bad news and I had told Frankie lots of times that she needed to move out. I even offered up my place but she couldn't leave Leah, said she needed her."

"What do you mean Leah needed Frankie? Did she mention what for or what was going on at all?" Geoff jumped into the conversation, intrigued by what the man had said. Perhaps this was a break in the case and they were about to get a real lead. Then again, considering the source and the fact he agreed with Andrews about Jason being on something, his confession probably wouldn't hold up in court or even with the captain.

"I don't know much more than that, Frankie never really talked about it. She was scared for Leah though, said she was in over her head and hoped she'd get a conscious before something bad happened." Jason looked between the two detectives. "Honestly, that's all I know. Frankie was a good person; she wouldn't be into anything bad herself. That's just not her."

"Where were you January eighteenth around nine am in the morning?" Andrews took the control back and intently watched Jason waiting for an answer.

He thought about it for a little and then slowly answered, "I was meditating, you can call my roommate to check, he was home as well."

Closing up the file, Andrews stood from her chair. "Thank you very much Mr. Banner. Please let us know if you think of anything else that would be helpful and for now please do not leave town. Thank you for your cooperation, you are free to go."

She sat back down as Baker ushered the man out the door. Needing just a moment to herself, she sat with her head resting on her folded arms, atop the table. Today was a tad overwhelming, and even with having had the entire day to herself yesterday she felt like she could still use another one. Looking at the front page of the file after a few moments of silence, Andrews saw a friend of both girls was coming in next. She saw next to Jason's name it had him listed as a creative writing major, which explained a lot.

There was a knock on the door and Andrews looked up to see her partner leading in a young woman. Assuming this was Julia; Andrews stood and pointed toward the chair across from her offering her to take a seat. "Thank you for coming in Ms. Miller."

"Oh, I would do anything to help you catch the guy that did this. Those girls were so sweet and really wouldn't get themselves into any sort of trouble. I can't even imagine why someone would pick them." She wiped a tear from her eye and looked at Andrews as though she were waiting for all the answers.

"I'm sorry Julia; I can't tell you why any of it happened yet, but I am hoping you'll be able to help us figure that out here today. Can you tell me about the relationship between Frankie and Leah?" Andrews really did wish she could help the poor girl out but there really wasn't much that they knew yet.

Julia smiled as she remembered the two girls, "They were more like sisters, but silent sisters. If something was ever wrong with Leah or Frankie the other one would be there and try to help but silently. They didn't really go out much; it was more of just supporting each other than anything else."

Andrews wrote down what the girl had told her, "Did you know of any problems between the two of them? Or any trouble that Leah might have been in?"

The smile from Julia's face slowly faded and concern replaced it. "Leah was in a relationship with an older man, and Frankie didn't approve at all. I don't know who it was, or anything about him. I just remember them fighting about it. Frankie wanted Leah to end it, but Leah claimed she was in love and that he was going to leave his wife for her."

"Did either of them say anything to you about it?" Andrews knew the story all too well. A young pretty girl came in and disrupted a marriage, the man claimed he loved her and that he would leave his wife and then the wife would find out and the girl would have to disappear so she couldn't cause trouble.

"No, I only just overheard the arguments." Julia got a look of confusion on her face, "Do you think that's why this happened? Is it because Leah was seeing a married man?"

"I'm sorry Julia we can't say for sure yet, but can you think of anything else that might be helpful or that seemed unusual in the past week or so?" Geoff had brought himself out of the shadows and came to stand next to the young woman.

Silence filled the room as Julia thought and the detectives patiently waited. Finally, she broke it, "No, I don't think there is."

Geoff moved toward the door and opened it. "Thank you for your cooperation Ms. Miller. If you think of anything please let us know."

As she got up and walked out the door, Geoff hovered and watched his partner staring off into space. He told her to sit still for a little and he'll bring in lunch in before the next person showed up. He assumed she had heard him, but he couldn't really be sure, there was no acknowledgement. Letting the door shut behind him, he made his way down the hall, pointed Ms. Miller in the right direction and then went over to his desk and grabbed the paper bag sitting there. Geoff headed back to the interrogation room and unloaded the bag of Chinese onto the table, handing his partner a pair of chopsticks.

"Thanks for getting lunch, I'm starving." She grabbed one of the points and opened it to see what was inside. "When does the next one show up?"

He slid the folder over to his side and flipped it open, "Looks like one of the campus officer's is coming in next and that's not for a half hour yet, we're ok on time." He saw her nod and start to drift off again, "Don't worry there's only two more of these and then we need to check in with Norm and that'll be it for the day."

She stuffed some Lo Mein into her mouth, and just smiled apologetically at her partner. Andrews knew she was being a wet rag and knew she could be helping Geoff out a little more. "Sounds good."

They ate quietly and passed the folder back and forth constantly point out different things without using words. It wasn't long before Geoff's phone started ringing and he picked up nodding to Andrews that it was time to start again. He quickly repacked the paper bag and told her that she could take the leftovers that his wife doesn't allow Chinese in the house, she thinks it smells. Andrews just chuckled and thanked him.

As had been the process all day, out went Baker and in coming Baker with some stranger. This time, however, it was someone in uniform, naturally it would have to be the campus officer. Andrews had evacuated her chair and decided to let Geoff conduct this interrogation. She felt that perhaps a detective that had been on the force for more than a few years would come off as more respectable than one still considered a rookie by some officers. Geoff had the same idea as he sat down opposite the officer.

"Lieutenant Lewis, I would like you to meet my partner, Detective Andrews, and again I would like to thank you for taking time out of your schedule to come down to help us." Geoff wasn't sure how much the UB officer could help with but it was better to talk to him and then not and possibly have missed something.

The lieutenant nodded in an Andrews' direction. "Nice to meet you and really Baker it's not a problem. What can I help you with?"

Opening up the file, Baker pulled out a school photo of each of the girls and put it in front of the officer. "Do you know about Leah Kummer and Frankie Gerald?"

"Those were the girls murdered over at Creekside village. I was on duty when you guys showed up and found the second girl." Lieutenant Robby Lewis picked up each of the photos and shook his head. He was nearing retirement and had actually left the Syracuse Police force and signed on with the university thinking it would be less dangerous and eventful. He realized though that it's a college campus and something is always happening that needs the police to be present.

"Did you hear anything strange that night or see anything at all? One of our officers had checked in with you before and found that no one had called about any noises." Geoff took the pictures back and returned them to the file.

He shook his head, "No, we didn't get reports about anything. Everything is still rather calm here because it's the start of the new semester. There hasn't really been any crime reported at all lately."

Geoff rubbed his forehead in frustration, "I honestly don't know what to do. No one saw or heard anything, on the entire campus. I find that really difficult to believe."

"Have you tried their CA? If someone in their complex had an issue with noise, they probably would have told the CA before anyone else. Most college students don't have the time or desire to stop by and talk to us when something is going wrong. They only come to us when something is stolen, or their car has been hit. Can't say it's ever really about noise, or domestic disturbances," Robby pointed out.

"I actually think that's who's coming in after you. Hopefully someone did go to her with something." Geoff stood as he offered his thanks, "Please let us know if anything turns up or you get any calls. Thank you again for your cooperation in our investigation."

The two men shook hands and Geoff opened the door to let the Lieutenant out and found a young woman standing there. She looked scared and began to shake when she saw the UB officer leaving the room. Geoff motioned for Andrews to come over to the door. They quickly exchanged a glance and Andrews knew it was her job to calm the girl down while her partner walked the officer out.

"Hi, you must be Lina Yang?" Andrews gently puts her hand on the woman's shoulder and gave a push to get her into the room. The girl didn't speak, but nodded between shakes. "Would you like to have a seat? And you know you're not in trouble, right?"

"Yes, I know I not in trouble. It is just so sad about the girls." Lina took a few deep breaths and started to calm down.

Andrews just looked at the girl and questioned how she got to be in college, and then she remembered that UB hosts students from around the world. "Are you an international student Lina?"

The woman nodded violently, "Yes, yes I am. Thank you for asking me. My English is good, no?"

"Is your English is good." Considering she was from another country and they do say English is the hardest language to learn, she was quite impressed. Andrews was about to ask another question, but Geoff walked in at that moment. He simply nodded and went to lean against the glass on the back wall.

Andrews opened the file and pulled the pictures of the victims from its showing Ms. Yang. "Lina, these girls lived in your building correct? You were their CA?"

"Yes, that is Leah and Frankie." The words were thick with her accent. "They nice girls and very clean."

"Do you remember anyone complaining about noise coming from their apartment at all this week or last week? Did anyone come to you saying they saw someone strange leaving the apartment?" Andrews didn't want to insult the girl, but she wasn't sure how good her English was, so she tried to keep things simple.

Lina looked at the table, searching for something to tell the detectives. "Nothing was said to me about them being loud. There were no strangers in the building; you need a pass card to get in."

"How would you describe the two girls and their relationship with the other people at Creekside?" Andrews had a feeling this was a dead end; no one had seen anything or heard anything.

"Nice, they, like everyone and everyone likes them. Leah was never home and Frankie had the boy over a lot, but I have not seen them since the weekend last." Lina nodded her head in confirmation of what she said.

Sighing, "Ok is there anything that you can tell us? Anything unusual at all?" Andrews was out of questions for the student.

Lina went to answer, but instead the tears just started falling and the shaking started up again. "No!" She continued to sob, "It wa-as, all, m-my fa-ault."

Andrews turned and looked at Geoff, being comforting wasn't a strong suit of hers. There really wasn't anything about her that was motherly and she really had no idea what to do. The woman in front of her was in complete hysterics now; she was saying something but no longer in English. Even if it was in English, Andrews was pretty sure she wouldn't be able to understand a word of it.

Thankfully Geoff came to the rescue as he moved away from the back wall. Helping the woman up, he leads her out the door comforting her as he went, "There, there child. It wasn't your fault and you won't lose your job or anything else. Everything will be ok, you'll see. Here's my card if you do, think of something later on, just give me a call anytime."

She was glad to be done with the questioning; spending a day in that room was more than enough. Andrews and Geoff had worked out a system, though, do all the questioning in one day, follow up on any leads that come of it and cross check stories and then get out in the field the rest of the time and actually catch the bad guy instead of staying in the room. Following the pair in front of her out into the lobby of the station, they both sent the hysterical CA on her way and then returned to their desks.

It was nice to finally be able to relax and the two just sat in silence, looking over their notes and swapping papers once in a while. The phone ringing interrupted their thinking and Geoff picked up. "Baker." He listened and smiled at his partner while nodding to the person on the other side of the line. He hung up, "Norm wants to see us."

The two made their way down to the "crypt" of the building. The detectives had labeled it such because it was the last place they wanted to ever go. The captain required each detective to talk with the medical examiner when a homicide was involved in the case however so they all have been down there at least once. Baker had gotten used to the whole crypt, but Andrews still grew a little queasy every time she went down there.

Norm was waiting for them when they arrived, "Ah, you're finally here. Well, I have a lot to tell you. "He walked over to the first gurney with Leah laid out anatomically on it and covered with a sheet.

"Norm, instead of doing the scientific talk and then having me ask you to repeat everything; can you just give it to me in plain English first place?" Geoff knew he wasn't as smart as his friend; he wanted to be able to understand what the man was saying instead of just nodding his head at him.

"Leah was our first victim, I took her temperature and it looks like she died approximately at eight am Tuesday morning. There are no markings on her or anything else that suggests a struggle, simply this contusions around her neck from someone strangling her." He pointed to the purple marks outlining the girls' neck acting as a choker. "I can also tell you that her attacker was taller than she was because of the angle the hyoid bone was broken."

"Well, how tall was Leah?" Andrews was doing her best to not look at the bodies, but just write down everything the medical examiner told her.

Norm walked over and checked his chart, "Seems that she was five six."

The detectives followed Norm over to the other body, "Frankie is the complete opposite of Leah. She shows that she did put up a struggle. There are bruises covering her entire body, as well as a hand print on her wrists. Dear Frankie was struck on her temporal with a hard square object. I have timed her death to be between nine and ten am on the same day."

"Is there anything else you can tell us about either of the girls?" Geoff looked over to his partner and made sure she was keeping up with the notes.

"Well, I did find some hair on both of their clothes as well as some other things I sent to the lab. There was this one thing though that I found to be very odd." Norm trailed off and started staring off into space.

Geoff walked over to face his friend, "Norm, what's with the look? What is it that you found?"

The man stroked his chin, "I found both their throats to be raw and with dry blood and stomach acids coating it. It was as though they had thrown up before dying. That made me curious, of course, because there was no regurgitation found at either scene. I looked at their stomach contents and then found something wildly interesting." He paused to go get his chart again.

"Come on Dr. Vance, you've got me really intrigued and that normally doesn't happen down here in the crypt." Andrews was okay with admitting it, she was actually really excited about what he had to tell them.

"It appears our ladies enjoyed a last meal of worms before dying, or as they died. From what their mouths and throats looked like I would say it was forced on them and they didn't ask for it." He shook his head in disgust. Those poor girls didn't stand a chance, it was obvious that Frankie had been overpowered and it seemed that Leah had never seen it coming.

Both Geoff and Bethany looked at each other. "Wait, you're telling us that they literally ate worms? So it wasn't that they were just holding them, but they had ingested them as well?" Bethany looked at her partner wondering if this was fact or just a joke they were playing on her. They had done that before, tried to convince her that a victim had bitten off his own toes and fingers. It was a known fact she had a weak stomach and the guys enjoyed using that to their advantage.

"Believe me, I am not joking. I sent the worms that had been in their hands and the whole ones I could pick out of their stomachs over to Frank. Perhaps he'll be able to tell you where the worms came from through the dirt." Norm went and sat at his desk that was against the wall. "I'm sorry guys but that's all I can give you for now. I need more time to let the bodies talk to me."

"It's okay buddy. Let us know if you find anything else, we'll leave you be for now." Geoff grabbed Andrews by the sleeve and dragged her with him as he left the crypt.

They walked back up the stairs both thinking about what they had been told. Half way up Andrews stopped and turned to Baker, "He really wasn't kidding was he?"

Baker just looked at her exhausted, "No, I don't think he was. Those girls really were forced to eat worms and then they were killed. I just really hope Frank can tell us something about them."

"Why would someone do that though, it's not at all normal. I wouldn't even think to feed a victim worms before finishing them off, that's just cruel and unusual." Andrews felt herself growing angry at the idea as well as a little nauseous.

"Look, it's nearing supper and my wife has already been harassing me about working so much. She doesn't seem to care that we're after a murderer, so I need to get home. Don't forget though we have that meeting with the therapist in the morning! Our weekly dose of fun!" Sarcasm just poured from his lips as he was discussing their shrink time.

"Sounds good, I'm going to hit the gym up first and then go crash." Andrews was glad to be going home and she was really glad that Baker hadn't invited her home with him for dinner. She always had problems saying no to him.

They reached their desks, updated the white board with the facts on the girls they had just received from Norm and then packed up. "Have a good night Bethany; I'll see you in the morning!" Geoff called as he walked toward the front door.

Bethany started heading for the door herself but then heard someone calling her name from behind. Turning she saw it was the captain and her hopes of getting home early fell. She changed her direction and instead made her way toward the captain's office. "You called?"

"Have a seat please, I'll keep it brief." Captain Harris definitely was not in the joking mood, it was all business tonight. "I heard Kevin came up while talking to the first victim's parents. You going to be able to handle this?"

"Yes sir, I can keep my emotions out of work. I haven't seen him in months and it's over between us. There is nothing to worry about, honest." This was the last thing she wanted to talk to her boss about.

Harris wasn't necessarily convinced but he couldn't hold her there till he made her talk. He knew they would be talking to Miranda in the morning so perhaps it would come out then. "Alright Bethany, you're free to leave." He would never admit it if questioned but that was the real reason he scheduled those two weekly sessions with the shrink. It helped him keep track of how Andrews was handling things better.

"See you tomorrow captain." Bethany excused herself and left his office. She made her way out the door and to her car without any more interruptions. On her way out she did wave good bye to the rookie officer from the first day, Junior.

She drove to the gym and just sitting in the parking lot decided she was too tired to do anything. Bethany turned the car around and headed back to her apartment. Going to the fridge, she looked in and saw nothing that caught her eye. Mother had always said if nothing jumps out at you then apparently you aren't hungry enough to eat. Instead of eating, she decided just to take a warm bubble bath and get to bed early. Something inside of her was warning her that tomorrow was going to be a really stressful day.

It was nights like this that she wished she was still living with Kevin. He was the best at just holding her and making the bad day fade away. She may not be able to admit it out loud but she truly did miss him and wanted the ability to just call him up and tell him everything, begging him to come back into her life. Bethany knew though her uncle would kill her himself if she ever contacted anyone from back home. She knew though the time was coming when she just wouldn't care anymore and she'd make the call, either to Kevin or her best friend Skylar. She just needed someone to talk to that knew who she really was and not this fake person she had created. Tonight however she would continue to listen and be the good girl, but she made no promises for tomorrow.

Chapter 3: Megadrile

"Andrews, Baker get to Dr. Shetty's office these sessions are not up for debate." Captain Harris glared at his two detectives.

No one particularly liked going to see Dr. Shetty. She was a fierce petite Indian woman. All she did was ask about feelings and how something made them feel. Andrews especially did not enjoy these visits. The woman would ask about her family, and because of the current situation, Andrews wasn't exactly allowed to tell the truth.

"Come on Bethany!" Remember the last time we were late? She made us role play. I'm fifty seven years old; my role playing days should be over." Baker's eyes smiled at her. He wasn't dumb he knew his partner dragged her feet because of some secret.

She shook her head, "I'm coming, I'm coming." Walking next to her partner as they made their way down the hall, she leaned in just outside the door. "Want to have some fun today? We have two murdered girls and really no suspects we need to get to work not have 'feeling time'".

"Alright, I'm in. What did you have in mind?" He raised his eyebrows at the woman when she walked into the office instead of answering him.

"Ah, you're late but come in." A brightly dressed woman sat tapping her pen behind a desk. In her mid-forties Miranda Shetty was a second generation Indian-American. She had no accent unless angered and on a rant, then her family's culture would coat every word. Once she had owned her own practice but working for the police gave her a different kind of excitement than the normal every day whack-jobs.

"Dr. Shetty," Andrews moved to sit, "my partner hasn't been making my coffee right. " She turned to face Baker. "I feel angry, when you put cream in my coffee and you know darn well I take it black."

Baker took the cue, "Well I feel frustrated when you leave the car keys on my desk and don't put them back in the drawer." His eyes were laughing but he tried his best to keep a straight face.

"Well, I feel rejected when you go to lunch and don't ask if I want to join you." Andrews placed her hands on her hips and gave a little attitude.

Knocking on her desk, drawing their attention back to her, Dr. Shetty rubbed her forehead. "Are you children done or would you like to waste more time and stay here longer?"

"This is ridiculous Miranda. Just ask us what you need to and let us get back to our jobs." Last thing Baker wanted was to spend all day in the shrink's office.

"You both are currently working on a double homicide, and you were both the first on the scene for the second murder." She paused giving herself time to read their expressions. "Are either of you struggling with this at all? Any issues with depression, nightmares or bouts of anger?"

Andrews rolled her eyes; it's the same questions every time. "No, no, no, and no. What I currently am struggling with is my building irritation of not being able to work on my case."

Baker felt the same as his partner but he had seen what cases could do to someone. He understood the need to at least have an opportunity to talk it out. One of the men on the force committed suicide because the stress of the case got to be too much.

"Ok well, Geoff you can leave, the captain would like me to talk to Bethany about some confidential matters.

Geoff exited the office giving his partner a sympathetic glance. It wasn't much but Andrews appreciated it. She had a feeling she wasn't going to like this conversation, though she couldn't understand why the captain would even tell Dr. Shetty.

"So doctor, what would you like to discuss? Where to get cheap shoes? What type of hair products works best?" Sure, she was smothering her words with sarcasm but it was keeping her from, lashing out.

Miranda pulled a folder from under a stack of papers. "The captain couldn't really tell me anything. He just wants me to make sure you adjusted well and to see if there are any problems or something you'd care to discuss."

"Look, I appreciate the thought and you all checking to make sure I'm not going to snap." She sighed heavily. "Really though it's all unnecessary. I'm fine. I've accepted my situation and let it go."

"What have you done other than work since you got here?" Dr. Shetty knew she wasn't going to get a thing from Bethany. She was obligated to try though.

"I go to the gym twice a week for kickboxing. Geoff and Val invite me over for dinner some nights." Andrews knew she really had no life; to her there was no point in getting one either.

The doctor pushed her pen into the pad of paper in front of her and drew some spirals. It was a good technique to fool the patient into thinking she was actually writing it down. Captain Harris had asked her to keep it all off the record though and completely confidential.

"What about dating, Bethany? You're a young, attractive, single female. Do you go on any dates?'

She snickered at the doctor's question. "Don't know if you realize but my job doesn't really allow for dating. I was engaged back home but that ended rather abruptly, so no I don't date."

"Is that something you're like to discuss? Perhaps we can get to the root of why it was so abrupt."

"No, plain and simple." Andrews stood up and walked over to the door grabbing hold of the handle.

Dr. Shetty knew the session was over and she had to let the detective go. Andrews apparently wasn't ready to talk yet. She had no idea though what she was going to tell the captain. "You may go Bethany, but my door is always open when you're ready to talk."

"Thanks, it's noted." With a last look around the earth themed room, Andrews left and made her way back to her desk.

Geoff was watching intently as his partner returned to her desk. She immediately put her head down and closed her eyes. He took that to be a sign it didn't go well and decided to let her have a moment to herself.

"Don't ask Baker." Andrews felt his eyes watching her.

"No need to snap, I wasn't going to."

She raised her head to apologize, "I'm sorry Geoff that was rude of me." Sitting all the way up, she spun her chair to face the board. "So where do we stand?"

Before Geoff could answer, Captain Harris stuck his head out the door. "Andrews, my office, now."

"Fabulous," she mumbled exasperated.

"What the heck is going on with you?" Geoff was becoming genuinely concerned for his partner.

Andrews glanced over at him and say the emotion in his face. "I wish I could tell you. Make all this a whole lot easier if I could."

The captain was anxiously waiting as she entered his office. "You got another letter from your admirer. I intercepted it when it came in. It was attached to a black rose."

"Oh, well black may be my color but anyone that knows me would never send a rose. Way too cliché."

"Andrews shut up and just sit down and listen." He picked up a small card off his desk. "In three days I will have my revenge. Love, your secret admirer," he read.

She rolled her eyes. "Aw, Corey sends his love from jail. How sweet of him."

Ignoring her last comment the captain continued his thought process. "I think it's time we told Baker, he has the right to know and with your life in danger his is as well." He picked up the phone, punched in a few numbers and ordered Baker into his office.

"Captain you want to see me?" Geoff looked from the captain to Bethany, waiting for an explanation.

Nodding, Captain Harris directed the detective to the empty seat next to his partner. "Have a seat; Bethany has something she needs to tell you."

"Way to throw me under the bus captain." She turned to face her partner and friend. "Back in Pa, I shot the brother of a drug dealer. The dealer then put a hit on me and my chief, who unfortunately is also my uncle, sent me here. No one but the chief and captain know about it. I never said goodbye just moved. Recently though I've been receiving letters from someone threatening my life."

"Wait. That's why you haven't talked about your family and why you got so weird about seeing your fiancé's picture in the Leah's house?" Geoff was mentally fitting the pieces together.

Captain Harris held up a hand, "Andrews, your fiancé knows our victim?"

"Yes. I saw him standing with our victim in one of the pictures on the mantle."

"You realize he'll be up here for the funeral? If he sees you or the parents mention your name this will cause more trouble for you." The captain scrunched his face in thought, trying to think up possible ways to avoid this becoming an issue.

Andrews tangled her hair around her fingers. "Yes, I realize that. I will take care of it. Now that Geoff knows he can help run interference."

"I'm not running anything till you explain a little more. So you have a partner back home that you just ditched without any true explanation? Was that what you were planning to do to me?" Baker was highly offended. He thought they had become close these past few months and yet he really knew nothing about his so-called partner.

"Jake is fine, he rebounded well so I'm told. I wasn't going to just run out on you, Geoff. My uncle didn't give me an option on the matter. Even my own mother didn't know." Bethany's voice began to rise in anger. This wouldn't be happening if she had been permitted to stay in Colebrookdale.

"If not even your mother knew then how did this guy know where to send the letters." Geoff was just a little confused.

Captain Harris fielded his question, "Pete and I aren't sure yet but we believe someone followed Andrews here."

"Captain you don't know that yet. You can't assume someone followed me just because you have two letters that some freak wrote." She didn't want anyone to start panicking just because something bad might be happening, it wasn't a definite thing.

Geoff was still confused and trying to piece everything together. "Why do you think someone followed her here? Is it because of the letters?"

"Yes Baker. The first one she received was about how this person had found her and was going to kill her and now they gave her a time, three days, before they take their revenge. We're actually considering sending her back to Colebrookdale so her uncle can better protect her. In a small town like that an outsider would be easily spotted." Captain Harris searched for transfer papers in his desk.

"Wait up, I'm not leaving." Bethany looked over at Geoff and then back at the captain, "I can't leave my partner. We're in the middle of a case."

Geoff's face dropped of all emotion, "Oh go ahead Bethany, and you left your first partner why shouldn't I be next?"

"Now that's not fair Geoff! I had no choice in the matter!" She grew frustrated at how this all of a sudden became her fault. She wasn't the one that told Corey to put a hit on her, she didn't tell her uncle to ship her off to another city and not tell anyone.

The captain stopped looking for the papers; he looked between both his detectives and sighed. "Obviously you two need to talk, I'll put a few guys on your case just for a few hours. Go get some coffee or something and talk this out. You need to have it settled or you're going to be a risk for each other while working your case."

"You might as well just fill me in Bethany. Let's go grab lunch and then we'll come back and work on the case more. Deal?" Geoff was hopeful, he wanted an open partnership. If he couldn't trust her then how would he know she'd take a bullet for him?

"Yeah, it's a deal."

The two detectives exited the office. Baker grabbed his keys off his desk and they headed to the squad car. On the way to their usual stop Bill Gray's, Bethany recognized one of the cars in front of them. Scooting down in her seat she attempted to disappear below the windshield.

"You ok Andrews?" Geoff was eyeing his partner, questioning her actions.

She smiled nervously back at him, "Yeah, know how my ex whatever you want to call him is our victim's cousin? Well, that's his car in front of us."

"Oh really," Geoff got a sly look on his face and started driving a little fast and moved into the other lane so he could pull up alongside him.

"Geoff Baker! Are you an idiot! What the heck!" Andrews scooted down even farther so soon she was out of her seatbelt and sitting on the floor.

"Andrews you realize you're breaking the law right now? Look, he's gone you can get back in your seat and buckle up!" Geoff was highly amused by how childish his partner had gotten within a few seconds.

She got back in her seat and buckled up while glaring at her partner. "I can't believe you." She paused when Geoff started pointing at her, but then she realized he was pointing past her and she turned her head to look out the window. "Kevin."

The man in the car next to them looked over at the same time and a look of shock consumed his expression. He was looking at his past and didn't believe what he was seeing for a moment. There was no way what he was seeing was real, she couldn't be there. After all this time of searching, she had been in Buffalo. Kevin shook it off though; he had been seeing her face everywhere since she disappeared. This was just another woman that looked like his girl and he'd pursue it and then find out it's not her and feel hopeless all over again. Not this time, his family was right, it was time to start letting go. He was here for his cousin's funeral anyways, not to chase a dream.

Andrews was confused but the look Kevin had given her. "I don't think he believed it was me. He looked at me like I didn't exist." She wasn't sure why, but she was actually hurt by the whole situation.

"What did you want him to do Bethany? Roll down the window and scream how much he missed you and wanted you back?" Geoff guessed he just didn't understand the whole romance thing anymore. He'd been married to his wife for over thirty years and back when he was courting her things were very different.

"You know what; I'm not really hungry anymore. Can you just go in a drive through somewhere and grab something to take back? We'll work on the board while we eat." Andrews pushed with a pleading tone.

Geoff didn't quite understand the need and it defeated the purpose of the captain sending them out to talk but he could tell she was upset so he complied. "Whatever you want Andrews."

They stopped and picked up Subway and then headed back to the station. Andrews kept her eyes peeled for Kevin even though she knew he was probably in Clarence by now at his aunt and uncle's house. Emotions she hadn't felt in a while were flooding back and she was realizing she didn't quite know how to handle them anymore. What she really wanted was to go over there and pull Kevin aside and talk to him and explain everything, but she knew he'd probably never forgive her. Plus, now that she had a taste of independence again, she wasn't quite ready to let that go.

Arriving back at the station the two detectives set up shop at their desks. Andrews plopped herself on top her desk and turned to face the board behind them. The two victim's pictures were taped to the board with descriptions of them both as well as where they were found and in what condition. On the other side of the board were the list of people they had questioned and then the words older man with a big question mark behind it.

"Geoff, we ever figure out who the older man was that Leah was seeing?" Andrews didn't remember hearing him mention anything but she had gone home early yesterday. Knowing Baker he probably came back to the station at some point after dinner to catch up on paperwork and follow up on whatever leads they had from earlier.

Geoff looked up from his lunch and over at the board. "Uh, no I don't think so actually. Why you have an idea?"

"No, I was just curious."

"Look, Bethany. I realize you don't want to talk about it but can you please just tell me what is going on with you? I want to be able to trust you but I can't do that if I don't know what is happening. If someone is after you, and you're with me almost all the time, that puts me in danger too. Valerie isn't going to appreciate me being in danger when I'm so close to retirement. I was going to retire a few months ago but then the captain asked me to do him a favor and be your partner for a little, you owe me an explanation." Geoff didn't mean to be cruel or anything but he really felt like he deserved to know why he was asked to hold off on his retirement.

Bethany really didn't want to but she felt bad for the guy, she had been lying to him for a while now. "Alright I'm sorry first off; I didn't mean to keep this from you." She got down from her desk and sat in her chair before rolling over to Geoff's desk so she wouldn't have to talk so loud.

"Andrews we're going to go in from the left, I want you to cover me." Harrison whispered to his partner as they both crouched down behind the door. "You ready?"

She just nodded toward him and held her gun out in front of her. Holding up another finger as she counted silently to three, Andrews reached up for the doorknob and slowly turned it. She opened it up just enough for Jake to slip through and then followed her partner into the warehouse. Her ears perked up as she could hear hushed tones, discussing a deal in the far corner. For months now they had been after this group of drug dealers. They were housed in the city of Reading but started selling to the high school students in her small town. Together the different police forces teamed up to bring down the drug ring and to put the leader Corey in jail finally.

Jake Harrison grabbed Bethany's sleeve and pulled her closer to him making sure to stay in front of her protectively. "Stay behind me!" he hissed at her.

"Shut up Jake, I'm not doing anything!" Bethany hated when he treated her like she was five. Yeah she was new to the force but this wasn't her first bust. Being on the Colebrookdale Police force meant she didn't really get a lot of action dealing with drug dealers or anything with extreme criminal activity so when the chance came along she'll admit she got a little over excited. This is why she joined after all, not to go around and arrest people for cow tipping or for crashing tractors.

"Just stay behind me Andrews; if you got shot I'd probably lose my badge. Let me go first, alright?" His eyes pleaded with her to just listen.

Andrews was stubborn, but she understood her partner's worry. If she ever got hurt her uncle, the chief would probably cause havoc on the rest of the force. "Fine."

The two moved along the shelves toward where they had heard the noise earlier. The voices were more muted then they had been before. Harrison waved for Andrews to go in front of him so she could cover his back, as he turned the corner. It was all clear and they continued moving along the shelves. As the neared the voices they could make out three distinct males ones. The deal was going down for some heroin as well as the hard stuff, crank. The detectives glanced at each other knowing they were both thinking about how if this stuff got out on the street they'd be busy trying to keep it out of the schools. That seemed to be the only probably with the small town, most of the kids hated living there and found it to be boring. To make up for that they tried to create their own excitement, all in the wrong way.

"Jake that's Corey, I'd know that voice anywhere." Andrews was furious. She and Corey had matched up a few times now and he always seemed to slip away. It was about time they cornered him.

He just nodded back at her confirming he had recognized the voice as well. The other two sounded familiar as well but he couldn't place them quite yet. Jake took a deep breath and then looked over at his partner. He thought he saw a glimpse of fear in her eyes but as quickly as it had come it disappeared. That girl was fearless, part of the whole reason being her partner scared him. It was time to make the move and they had to do this together or else it wouldn't turn out right.

Andrews knew why he was watching her; she was used to it though. "I'm ready. Let's do this."

"Are you sure? We can just hang out here till back-up comes; I am not at all against that idea." Harrison wanted to make sure she really was ready. Going in there without a plan could be deadly. Sure they had bulletproof vests on but at close range that really doesn't do much.

She smiled back at him trying to reassure him and calm his fears. Instead of trying to use words Andrews just held her gun out in front of her and put her game face on. She was ready, and had been ready for this for a long time. Taking the lead, she moved into position with her back against the shelf at the edge. Andrews closed her eyes and pumped herself up; opening them again, she saw Harrison had moved into place as well.

Holding out his fist Jake offered their ritual phrase, "I'll be seeing you."

"For a tall mocha latte," She whispered back

"It's a date." And with that Jake spun around the corner holding his gun out and screaming for the dealers to put their hands up.

Andrews followed announcing that they were the police. She watched as all three put their hands up but then looked at each other and all scattered at the same time. Both her and Jake fired and got the two they hadn't recognized in the leg causing them to fall down in place. Seeing Corey take off between the shelves she followed him and told Jake to watch the other two as she ran. Adrenaline pumped through her and she knew she couldn't let him get away yet again.

"Oh Bethany darling, didn't you want to play today? You should have called I would have put on my running shoes." Corey taunted her. He loved these cat and mouse games with her, added excitement to the dull routine of dealing.

She didn't want to waste her breath on talking to him but focused on even breaths to keep up with running. Andrews made it to the end of one of the aisles and saw she had hit a dead end. There was nowhere to go but back the way she came. As she started to turn she could hear someone breathing heavy behind her.

"Well, well, well. Ain't this just a conundrum for you beautiful?" Corey sneered at having her cornered.

Andrews turned to face the man, "What do you want Corey? What is so great about selling drugs to high schoolers?"

"It's not about the drugs, it's about the money. They all just get mommy and daddy's money for nothing, why shouldn't I offer to take it off their hands? It would be rude of me not to give them something for it then. Plus, they found me. I would have never thought to come to this town; it doesn't even exist on the map you know." He was enjoying watching her squirm. She didn't seem afraid but there certainly was something going on inside her.

Andrews put her gun down and held her hands up palms facing Corey. "You going to shoot me Corey? Add cop killer onto your list of crimes?"

He smiled at her, "I could never kill you. Where would the fun be in that? I enjoy our little games Detective Andrews."

"Then what do you want with me? I'm not holding my gun you can get away easily if you truly wanted." She was stalling. In the back of her mind she was really hoping that Jake would join them soon and then they would have Corey surrounded.

"What do I want with you? I'm afraid if I told you that I wouldn't be able to fantasize about surprising you anymore detective. That's half the fun." He'd admit it; he had a crush on her. Corey had been back and forth in these games since Andrews had joined the force. He really did enjoy their meetings.

Something fell behind where the two stood and Corey panicked. A gun went off and there was just a scattering of feet and voices yelling. In the distance someone was screaming a name but Andrews was frozen where she had stood. She looked down and saw her blouse was now stained. Touching the spot she felt a sharp pain travel through her body and she just collapsed from the agony.

"Andrews!" The voice was muffled but she heard it getting closer. Before blacking out she remembered the voice right by her ear, "I'm sorry detective. We'll finish this game later, get better soon."

Andrews sat straight up in bed and instantly put her hand where the bullet had struck her. It was a recurring nightmare anymore and she wished it would just leave her mind forever. Apparently telling

Geoff today about how she came to Buffalo brought up the memories. She knew she wouldn't be able to sleep now so she decided to just shower and get an early start to the day. Going into the bathroom, she stood in front of the mirror and lifted her shirt. Above her left hip was the scar. She touched it flinching at the memory of the pain. Those had been the longest six months of her life and she hoped she would never get shot again.

It was Corey's voice though that stayed with her the most from that night. She didn't quite remember what had happened but she definitely remembered what he had whispered in her ear. She also remembered her uncle coming down hard on her and sticking her on paperwork for a while. Of course Harrison had been a faithful annoying puppy the entire recovery process. She loved him for that but it really had annoyed her.

While looking at herself in the mirror, Andrews made the ultimate decision. With those letters and now this serial killer case, she wasn't going to stay hidden from her friends and family any longer. In that moment, she made the decision that today before work she was going to make the call to her best friend and just spill about everything. She needed someone to talk to or she was going to lose her mind. She couldn't keep this secret anymore, and now that Geoff knew the truth he was going to baby her and watch her even more.

Andrews hated people treating her like she was fragile. Yes, she was shot and yes, she now killed the brother of the man who had shot her. Of course there is the fact that now the man who had shot her was after here to get revenge for his brother's death. There was also the fact that her fiancé was the cousin of the first victim in her homicide case. Sure, her life was in danger and she was under emotional strain, so sure there was probable cause to treat her like she could break at any moment but she still hated when people did that.

66

Bethany went about her morning routine just a few hours sooner. She took her shower while singing songs of the best of the 80's, and then making herself a pizza omelet for breakfast. Unhealthy yes but the way she figured it, if people could eat cold pizza for breakfast why not just put the ingredients into eggs and make an omelet? Plus, it was unmentionably tasty. She decided to just stay in lounge wear till before she had to leave, might as well stay comfortable as long as possible.

She broke her trend then and went on the computer, something she hadn't done in a long time. Now she finally had the spare time though to check her personal email. Of course the moment she signs in a notice pops up telling her that she has forty unread messages. Bethany felt herself go into a cold, warm shock when she saw the newest one was from Kevin. The subject read, "I know that was you in the car. We need to talk." She didn't even need to open the message to know this wasn't going to end well. Now he knew where she was, it wouldn't take long at all for him to find her. For now, this would need to stay her little secret. The moment Geoff found out he would tell the captain and then she'd be off the case. And yet again the secrets began to build.

Chapter 4: Angleworm

Skylar had been thinking about her best friend the other day. She was working on her summer line already and getting the show ready. Bee had promised to be a model for the career wear but since the disappearing act, Skylar wasn't sure if she'd even ever talk to Bee again. She remembered how angry she had been the first week or so and then worry had taken over only to leave disappointment consuming all other emotions. She felt abandoned and working on this summer line knowing her best friend wasn't going to be there to support her like she promised made her ache.

Bee had been the one that named the company "Razz Designs". Growing up Bee and Skylar had been addicted to the Razzles candy, so one day Bee just started calling Skylar, Razz. The name eventually stuck and then "Razz Designs" was born. Skylar really did owe her success to her best friend and yet that's the one person that wouldn't be there for her this year. Skylar remembered helping Kevin with the search to find Bethany when she first vanished. It had broken both their hearts when nothing surfaced as the days passed.

She was deep in her own thoughts staring down at her sketch book when the phone rang. Skylar didn't feel like answering and just let the machine get it. As the beep rang through the room, Skylar started to cry when she heard the voice leaving the message. Without a moment's time of hesitance she ran and grabbed the phone. "Bee?" Her voice shook as she answered.

"Hey Razz, I was thinking about you this morning and thought I would try calling you. I hope that's ok?" Bethany was waiting for the eruption from her friend. Months of not talking to each other was bound to cause some sort of anger. She deserved it though.

The tears just continued falling as Skylar listened to her best friend talk to her through the phone. "Stop Bee," she paused trying to calm herself enough to get the next part out. "I just have one question for you."

"It's okay Sky, you can ask me anything." The waiting was killing her and Bethany was now starting to feel the tears building up in her eyes as well. She wasn't sure what the question was or what was coming next but she figured it could go either way, good or bad.

"Where are you? Why did you leave? What were you thinking leaving me like that?" Once she started asking questions, more flooded to her mind. All the questions she had been asking over the months escaped in such a fury, Skylar caught herself growing angry and frustrated all over again.

Bethany knew she couldn't answer any of those questions, all she could do was apologize and hope that maybe someday she could tell Skylar. "I'm sorry for leaving you, and I'm sorry for not telling you where I was or what I was doing. I can't tell you what's going on, for your own safety. I shouldn't have even called you, I just needed to hear your voice."

"Bee, I can't handle not knowing what happened to you. I thought you were dead for the longest time. Kevin hired investigators to find you, he searched himself and never found anything. You were dead to us, we even held a memorial. Why are you calling me now of all times. Why now?" She didn't want excuses, she made those up in her head. She wanted answers.

"Maybe this was a bad idea. Look Sky I'm sorry, I need to go. I'll call you and explain everything when this all gets settled. Till then please let my mom know I'm ok, and take care of her for me." That was all she could do for now and it was the hardest thing to have to say goodbye and not tell her best friend everything.

"What about Kevin, Bee?"

Bethany chuckled, "Don't worry Sky, Kevin already knows. He found me." That was something she was seriously going to avoid for as long as possible. "Bye Sky, I miss you." With that, she quickly hung up the phone and let the tears fall as she cradled the phone to her chest. Bethany had never felt so alone in her life. She knew she had done the right thing in keeping Skylar out of the loop for now. Telling her would put her in danger and being this far away, she couldn't protect her.

Checking the clock she saw it was nearing eleven. Bethany sighed knowing she had to start getting ready for work, she had promised Geoff she'd be in around noon. It didn't take her long to clean up and get over to the station. She had even made time to take her black lab Bailey for a quick walk. When she got to the station, Geoff was waiting for her by their desks just staring at the white board.

"Got any updates for me?" She walked over and joined him in front of the board.

He quickly glanced over and saw it was her, and then turned back. "Yes actually, found out the mystery man is a Karl Montgomery from the university. I have someone out getting him now."

"So what's his relation to our victims then? Was he Leah's boyfriend or was it something else?"

Geoff gave his partner his full attention, "Montgomery is a professor there and was Leah's faculty adviser. Seems he has a reputation for being too friendly with his students though."

Bethany just snickered at the comment. "Alright so, let's run over what we have as a timeline now and you can fill me in with whatever new you found out. Okay?"

He didn't answer her but simply handed her the dry-erase marker and pointed toward the board. Bethany moved to where the time line had started, March 7th, 2011 which was a Tuesday. "So we know that on Tuesday, Leah died around 8am and then Frankie was between 9 and 10 that same morning."

"I'm going to stop you there actually. Norm called this morning, the entomologists got back to him about the dirt found in each of the worms." Dramatic pause before he started again, "It seems that each individual worm had dirt ingested from a very specific and unique area of the entire state."

"You're not kidding, are you?" Andrews was confused slightly.

Baker shook his head, "Nope, I am not kidding. Whoever did this apparently knew we'd check the worms."

She glanced down for a moment and twisted the marker between her fingers. "You realize then that this was premeditated. Not just a few days but probably over the course of months if he did that much prepping for those murders. Unless he had help of course."

"I don't know, but either way we have a serious murderer out there with no true leads other than this professor." Baker went over to his desk and picked up his notepad he used in interrogations. "I checked out everyone we spoke too, all their alibis checked out. We really don't have anything right now."

As he said that his phone rang on the desk and his body sank down a little. Picking up he stated who he was and just listened. "What do you mean you can't find him?" Listening more he looked over at Andrews, his face strained with frustration. "Alright well ask when he'll be back from this vacation then, pass the word that we're looking for him and that I want him in here as soon as possible."

Andrews waited till he hung up the phone to question him, "What's going on?"

"Seems our professor has decided to take a spontaneous vacation, the officers I sent over couldn't find him." Geoff was not at all happy over the news.

"So what does that mean for us? Are we just supposed to sit here and wait for the good professor to get back from his vacation?" She hoped that would not be the case, but if he was gone what else could they do really?

Geoff smirked at his partner, "Well, how bout we find Mr. Montgomery and put an end to his vacation rather quickly. I can have officers out looking for him, and we can be home by 6 tonight yet. How does that sound?"

"I just love how your mind works Mr. Baker. Bailey and I had a date with Ben and Jerry tonight anyway." Andrews laughed at the confused look from her partner, so what if she had no social life the life she did have was nothing she was going to complain about.

"You are very strange my dear girl. A date with your dog and ice cream, only you."

She rolled her eyes and got off her desk, picking up the phone and resting it on her shoulder. "Start making your call buddy, I'll check with my contacts and see if I can help you track him down."

It took a few hours, but soon Dr. Karl Montgomery was waiting in the interrogation room. The two detectives stood behind the glass, watching their suspect. The man looks to be well into his sixties, with a full grown gray beard. He was dressed to the nines, either for show or he really was that rich. One thing missing however was his wedding ring. It had been mentioned that Leah was seeing a married man, not just an older one.

"He looks rather calm for a murder suspect, doesn't he Baker?" Andrews had been watching for the man to start tapping his fingers, or anxiously look toward the door. He did neither, he just sat there staring at the glass, patiently waiting.

Geoff looked over at his partner, "It's annoying, isn't it?" He sighed heavily and walked over to leave the room. "Well, let's get this interview over with. I need to get home on time, my daughter is stopping by with more wedding magazines or something. Only two more weeks to go and already my wallet was feeling empty."

"That's what daddies are for Geoff, making their daughter's dream day come true." Andrews was saddened thinking about how jealous she was of Geoff's daughter Michelle.

The two detectives entered the room where the professor was waiting. He never flinched, didn't look their way or acknowledge them in any way, he simply sat there. Geoff took the lead this time, taking his seat in the chair opposite Dr. Montgomery. The men exchanged glances before Geoff took out the picture he had of Leah and passed it across the table to Karl. The professor glanced down and picked up the photo. Andrews thought she had seen a look of sympathy cross the man's face, but as fast as it had appeared it was gone.

"Sir, were you aware that one of your students, Leah Kummer was murdered this past Tuesday?" Geoff waited for a response anxious to hear the professor's answer.

Dr. Montgomery looked up from the picture and straight into the detective's eyes. "I am only aware of what I have seen on the news and heard in passing from my colleagues."

"And what exactly would that be? What have your colleagues told you?"

"Not all that much," Montgomery thought for a moment. "They did mention the girl's body was found on a street corner somewhere."

Baker studied the man, "Anything else you can remember them telling you?"

"Now I believe that was all."

"And where exactly were you on Tuesday morning, sir?"

Almost smiling the professor once again folded his hands and slowly, as though questioning the intelligence of the detectives said, "I do believe it is my constitutional right to not answer any further questions before my attorney arrives. I believe I should also inform you that my attorney is on vacation

With his family in Vermont currently and will not be returning back to the state until early next week. I am terribly sorry for the inconvenience."

The man stood ushering himself out the door. "You may contact me with any other questions you might have through my attorney once he arrives home. Until then detectives, it was nice meeting you both and I really hope to never see either of you again. Good day to you both."

"Dr. Montgomery." Andrews spoke up and walked over to the door, holding it for the professor.

"Yes, detective?"

Andrews gave the same kind of smile she had just received back to the professor, "I am dreadfully sorry for needing to tell you this, but sadly you will be seeing us again. Professors who screw their students, who are later found dead, normally get to have a very long discussion with us. Good day to you as well, professor."

"I would be very careful who you upset these days detective, there could be a madman out there." Montgomery started walking away. "Free advice detective."

Dr. Montgomery left the room and walked down the hall. Baker stood from the desk and snickered at Andrews. "That went pretty well, don't you think?"

His partner rolled her eyes at him in response and started down the hallway. The two detectives decide to call it a night and meet up early the next day before their meeting with the entomologist at ten. They had already been warned that the chief will want an update tomorrow as well. Andrews wishes Baker a good night, excited she gets to go home and have a date night with Bailey.

Entering the apartment, Andrews is greeted by her black lab puppy. "Did you miss me Bailey? Well, I am home to stay tonight, so how about we get the human some ice cream and the dog some kibbles!"

Bailey wagged her tail furiously, following Bethany around the apartment as she put together their separate meals. Heading over to the couch, Bee looks over her DVD selection, along the wall and grabs for "Kiss the Girls". She figured watching someone actually solve a case might be a good encouragement to solve her own, it also served as a highly entertaining distraction from her own case. Pulling the files from her briefcase, she opened them up and started going over the photos from the scenes.

Bethany kept going back and forth between the movie and her own case. Something about the fetish killer in the movie was making her think there was another angle to the girls' murders. She went over in her head what she remembered about fetish killers and how they operate. Her professor in college used to talk about the difference between sociopaths and psychopaths and how the fetish killer is more of a psychopath because he can't help himself. Something triggers the reaction and the craving intensifies with each kill.

Picking up the crime scene photo from each of the murders, Bethany looked and realized the message was in the worms. Both scenes were drastically different. Leah never fought back, she either knew the person or didn't see it coming. Frankie though, wasn't such a clean kill, both girls though had the earthworm connection. That was her focus, now she just had to figure out what the worms represented. Bee grabbed the remote and turned up the movie so she could hear it as she walked around the apartment. After putting what was left of her ice cream back into the freezer, she headed for her bedroom with Bailey curiously following.

"Bubby, I do believe I am on to something", Bee exclaimed when she noticed her puppy close at her heels.

Changing quickly into pajamas, Bethany headed back out into the living room for her desk by the far wall. Grabbing at the Post-it note stacks and sharpie markers, she started throwing whatever was in reach in the direction of the couch. Bailey went over to the clutter of supplies collected on the couch and sniffed them, cringing as more came flying in her direction.

Bethany looked up from what she doing and saw the dog looking at her while was tilting her head, "Oh, I'm sorry Bailey, I didn't mean to hit you. You and I are going to figure this case out tonight! You can be my own personal Wish-Bone, crime fighting dog. How does that sound?" She laughed as her puppy laid on top of the sharpies and started rolling around. "You really are a strange dog, though that's probably why we get along so well."

She walked over to the couch, pushing her dog off the sharpies and started separating the markers from the Post-it notes. Just for fun she put each pile into a rainbow color scheme before pulling the coffee table closer to where she was now sitting on the floor, in front of the couch. Bailey made herself comfortable on the couch, sprawling out.

"A lot of help you'll be from up there Bubby." Bethany reached up and scratched her dog behind the ears. "Alright then, let's see what we can do."

Bethany uncapped one of the markers, putting it in her mouth and pulled a pad from off the floor. "Ok, so what type of fetishes involve worms? What type of anything involves an earthworm? Think Bee, think."

Lining up a few post-its on the table, she began to write down anything that came to mind associated with worms. "There's that inch worm on Sesame Street, fishermen use worms, lots of things like to eat worms. So that leaves a guy who likes to fish, watch cartoons and eat worms." She laughed at how ridiculous that sounded.

She grabbed another stack of Post-it notes, this time a different color and a new marker. "Ok Bailey, Leah and Frankie had a worm in their hand. Maybe Frankie wasn't such a clean kill because she struggled and the killer was worried about being heard so he left before he could finish posing her. Or maybe where the worms were having nothing to do with anything and how they died doesn't either. Maybe this won't help the case at all and I'm just wasting our time Bailey."

The television got louder as a chase scene began, "See, why can't it be that easy? They catch the killer within hours or days of what took place. Wouldn't it be nice if real life was more like the movies? You know what I would love Bailey? My own soundtrack to life, like out of a John Hughes movie." Looking over her shoulder at her puppy starting to fall asleep, she whispered softly, "I know what you're thinking Bailey, I got to find a man first. All those good movies have a man in them."

Turning back to her task at hand, Bethany again pulled another color of the Post-it notes and the sharpie markers. She wrote down common places people could obtain earthworms. The list ended up to be longer than she originally had expected and she crumpled up the ones that didn't suit the location of the campus or just the life in the city. There really weren't many places people could go to fish around Buffalo, especially while it was still cold.

Bethany sat back and watched the end portion of the movie, frustrated over worms. As the movie ended, she shut off the DVD player and switched the channel to the local news, WB on your side channel 2 news. She liked this program because it was about an hour earlier than most, so instead of having to stay up till eleven she just had to be up till ten. The first story of the night was of course about the two girls found murdered on the University's campus. Classes apparently had been canceled for the day in mourning over the loss of two students. There were candlelight vigils being held on the corner where Leah had been found, as well as, in front of the Creekside Village complex.

A few of the students were interviewed and told snit-bits about both girls and how they had loved life. Bethany wondered how much of that was true, that seemed to be the response to anyone dying, that they had loved life. Did they really enjoy life or is that all part of the grieving process to

78

create a false last memory and reality of the victim? Before going to commercial, the news reporter brought up a picture of an earthworm and mentioned police details being leaked to the public. The woman said she'd say more on the story next.

"Uh oh Bailey, someone is in big trouble for this. You're my alibi for tonight, if anyone asks I was with you the entire time." Bethany waited for the commercials to end, she knew not only the chief but Baker was going to be very upset tomorrow over this program. They had wanted to keep the worm detail out of the media just in case of copycats.

The news program came back on and again the picture of the earthworms was flashed up on the screen. "Tonight we have a chilling detail to add to the story of these two young college students murdered earlier this week. It seems along with each of the bodies, an earthworm was found as a calling card. Other sources in the media have chosen to nickname this man, Worm because of his unusual gift left behind at the scene. It is still unknown what connection this insect has with the women or with the killer. Stay tuned for updates on this case as it unfolds."

Bee shut off the television in disgust. That's exactly what the killer wanted, fame for what he has done. Most serial killers want the acknowledgement; even if they get caught, they are happy because they would get their name all over the news, in history books and known throughout the country. People would fear their name and that is what they love about being recognized, having control. Bethany knew they not only would the captain be upset, but Geoff would be too. This would make it harder to find the murderer now that the public knew the details of the case. Copycats could start their own runs, and the Buffalo public would no longer feel safe in their homes.

Overall, the media just made this case ten times worse than it had already been. Bethany had a feeling "Worm" would kick it up a notch in order to gain more fame. That was something they definitely did not need at the moment. Then again having it all out there for the public might help. Maybe someone saw something but never came forward. Andrews wasn't sure what the reaction would be but she was already dreading work tomorrow.

Chapter 5: Nightcrawler

Bee walked in the next morning and was greeted with a large coffee. "Here is your mocha iced frapp, which is nothing compared to my two cream, one sugar. You're basically drinking dessert for breakfast, not coffee." Geoff looked especially happy this morning, not something Bethany was expecting at all.

"Thank you very much, I needed this. Guess you saw the news program last night?" Bee was weary of what reaction she would get from her partner. Shockingly he didn't look too upset by it.

Geoff walked over to his desk and sat down, thumbing through some paperwork. "I did see it, and I think whoever leaked about the worms should be thrown into jail for making our jobs harder. There isn't anything we can do about it now. I guess being on the job for so long, it's taught me that somehow the media always finds out. It's inevitable really."

"I realize that, they are slimy in that way but still I thought you'd be a little more upset over the whole thing." Andrews paused wondering if she should tell him about what she had been thinking about last night. She should, he was her partner so even if he laughed at her it could at least spark something in his mind. "Hey Geoff, last night Bailey and I were going over the case. Do you think that maybe we should be focusing more on the worms than what we are? Even the media picked up that it was the unique part of the case."

"I see where you're going with that, well what did you and the puppy come up with?" He was listening to her, but also in his own mind thinking about the press release that would need to be done now that the media knew about the specific details. He was sure the captain would make him give it.

Andrews pulled out her sticky notes from the previous night and started reading them off to her partner, making sure not to make eye contact. "Well there's that worm on Sesame Street, and fisherman use worms, so they'd be in direct contact with them. There is also the possibility of him being like Frank, just a bug person? Ok look, I really don't know what is so damn important about those worms. I keep hearing that stupid nursery rhyme in my head about eating worms on the garden wall, or something crazy like that."

"You may actually be onto something." He spun his chair around and squinted his eyes in thought. "You know, we had a case a while back, before you were even on the force," he winked, "and there was a guy who would put a snake with each of his victims. Turned out he was just tired of them being in his garden and though that would be a more proper use for them. Perhaps this case is similar to that one."

"But in what way would your snake guy be like our worm guy? You mean that perhaps he's just sick of worms and so he covers his victims with them? Or do you think there's something more meaningful going on there?"

Taking a sip of coffee first, he nodded stalling before he had to say something and then lit up as an idea came into his head. "I think it's more personal than that. I was just thinking about that nursery song you have stuck in your head, what if that's what he's thinking about and so obsessed over?"

"You think that song is what this is all about?" Andrews was confused now, she was just joking about that whole idea.

"Yeah that is what I'm thinking. Do you happen to remember how the actual song goes?"

Andrews bobbed her head, humming the rhyme hoping the words would just come to her. "I think it's something like, 'everybody hates me, nobody love me I'm going to go eat worms. Big, fat squishy ones, long something something ones sitting on the garden wall. First you bite the head off then you suck the guts out and then you throw the skin away, something something.' Oh I don't remember. It's just about some kid feeling unloved and eating worms."

"Such a lovely song for little kids to grow up on." Geoff laughed remembering that it was his generation that had a few nursery rhymes with hidden meanings as well, like Ring Around the Rosie.

"So the girls died because they're hated? Is that the conclusion we are coming to?"

Baker looked at his partner questioningly, "You have worked on cases before right? People don't normally murder someone because they love them, there normally tends to be a shred of hatred in there somewhere."

"No kidding Sherlock, I'm just asking if perhaps these girls were murdered because of the meaning of the song. It wasn't a random thought about them being hated. I get that they weren't especially liked." Andrews chuckled at him, she loved that they could banter and be so openly honest with each other. Helped make working together for long hours easier.

"I can't say for sure that our murderer killed those girls while singing the song, but it is definitely a possibility."

The phone by Baker's desk rang. He scooted back his chair grabbing it as he rolled past. "Baker", he paused listening to the person on the other line, "Yes sir she is, yes sir we can be. Okay sir we will be right in, yes sir I will."

Questioningly, she asked her partner, "Was that the captain?"

"Yes, Andrews it was and I'm supposed to let you know that you're fired and you should pack your bags and go home. It seems they found your stash of chocolate and you're the reason we have mice so they are kicking you out!" Amused by his own joke, he laughed before grabbing the paperwork off his desk and standing. "Harris wants to see us about the case; he wanted to make sure you were here physically, and mentally."

"Figures."

"I told him you were, so don't let me down in there." He winked at his partner as she shot him a glare back.

The two detectives entered the captain's office, and were greeted with a wave of the hand. Geoff pulled out the one chair for Andrews and she curtsied before sitting down, laughing at his old fashioned habits. If only men still acted like that today, it was the same conversation she was having her dog not too long ago. There just aren't any good ones left. Andrews could tell from the look on captain Harris' face that good news was not going to come out first.

"I'm going to assume you both saw the news last night. We need to discuss how you're each going to handle it." Harris looked directly at Geoff, "With you being the senior officer, I'm going to assume you're the one to do the press conference? And you Andrews, you can be there but I don't suggest you saying anything."

Andrews tilted her head at the captain, "Is that because I'm a women, I'm young or do you just not think I could handle talking in front of a large group of people?" Raising her eyebrows she continued to question her boss, "Why can't I do the press conference?"

Captain Harris laughed at his detective, "Andrews you have a hit on your head in a different state and you've been getting love letters threatening your life, last thing you should be doing is going on public TV announcing where you are."

"Oh yeah, I forgot about that. Guess that would be a suicidal move. Well then," she patted her partner on the shoulder, "It's all up to you old man!"

Baker looked anything but thrilled, "Aren't you two nice. What exactly do you want me to say captain? Want to go with the notion of it being a mistake or is there another approach you think would be better suited?"

"I think for now we should just play along. It's already out there and the public knows. In order to keep the panic down, and to minimize the possibility of copycats lets neither confirm it nor deny it. See what happens first." The captain sighed out of frustration. "I don't know how the public is going to react to the media's news, talk to our PR person and see what they think."

"Alright, I can call Heather up." Baker took out his notepad and jotted it down so he could remind himself later to give her a call.

Leaning across his desk, the captain looked between Andrews and Baker, "what is the update on the case? Are you any closer to figuring out who did this than you were yesterday?"

Andrews spoke first, "Well we do have the new lead sir in the Kummer case, and it seems she was having an affair with her professor Dr. Karl Montgomery. We have yet to really get a hold of him though, he cried lawyer from day one." She looked over at her partner silently asking if she should mention what they had been talking about earlier.

Geoff nodded and turned to tell Harris their new theory. "Captain, do you remember that nursery rhyme about the kid who wasn't loved and thought everyone hated him so he went and ate worms? We were thinking that perhaps the victims were hated, or rather they were the bullies of this murderer who was the one that felt hated and this is his way of revenge."

Andrews stared at her partner. That wasn't exactly what they had talked about before but she could see the wheels turning in his head that he was drawing a new conclusion. To her it sounded a little more accurate than the one she had formulated earlier. It was more of a possibility that the killer had been the one that was hated and not the victims, but it was more of an attack on the victims.

"I see where you're going with that Baker and that is a good theory. You could work off that if this Karl Montgomery part doesn't fan out." The captain seemed to be forming his own ideas. "Maybe you should go back to Leah's friends and family and ask them if there was anyone she didn't particularly like. That may get you a good lead on the new theory."

"We can look into that after we talk to Karl, sir. I don't know how much more we can get out of him, though." Geoff was more anxious to get started back at the beginning. He remembered though that the professor's connection was with Leah so in a way he would get his chance to ask about the theory as well.

There was a vibration of a phone and Andrews looked down to check the caller id. It came up "Bug Guy" and she motioned to Geoff that they would have to go. "Captain Harris, as always it's a pleasure, though don't be shy to let me know when I can go home."

"Oh don't you worry Andrews, as soon as your uncle gives me the okay I will not hesitate to let you know and send you on your way back to the small town." He said it as stern as he could but he knew he really would miss her when the time came to say goodbye.

The two detectives left his office and headed toward Frank Burn's small corner of the department. He had a little hole in the basement where he could keep his specimens. Before he had been in a room on the first floor but after a mishap and a few escaped hissing cockroaches, the captain decided that perhaps he would be better off in the basement, away from other people who didn't necessarily enjoy insects. Andrews didn't particularly like going to see him. To her he was kind of like

Norm but with bugs instead of the dead. He ended up telling them more than they needed to know and nothing that was of use normally.

Reaching the basement, they see a single light on and a man hovering over a microscope. Frank was one of those people that reminded Andrews of the creepy uncle families tried to hide. It wasn't that she thought he would actually ever do something, but he gave a weird vibe. Andrews stayed behind Baker as they walked down to the lab. Her senses were on over load from the nauseating smells escaping the room. Jars and tanks lined the walls, filled with different annelids and insects. It was like walking into a bug mall, which disgusted Andrews. Frank was bent over a sliced worm, taking samples of the dirt and making up slides when they came closer.

"Frank, are you finding anything of interest?" Baker spoke as they entered. He thought that'd be better than scaring the scientist, who was deep in his work.

The man looked up over his glasses, "Ah, hello officers. I see you got my call, you hadn't answered so I wasn't sure if you'd come."

"We were in a meeting with the chief, Burns, I saw your number on my caller ID though." Andrews though she caught the man sneering, chills ran through her body. This guy really did give her the wrong vibes.

The entomologist got up and grabbed his notebook from the desk. Handing it to Baker he began to explain. "I took some dirty from each of the worms found at the crime scenes. Looking under the microscope at the slides, I found that each worm had fed on dirt from a different location."

Baker handed the report over to Andrews to look at as Frank continued, "No two worms were at the same location before being placed in the girls' hands or in their throat."

"Is it possible for you to narrow it down and give us an exact location based off this?" Baker was pretty sure that was possible. It was a stretch but could really end up being invaluable information.

Frank beamed, "not just any person could tell you, but lucky for you I can. I want to work on it a little more and then get back to you."

"Just call when you know then." Andrews was anxious to leave. She pulled at her partner's shirt, attempting to pass along the hint that she was ready to get out of there.

Baker took the report from Andrews and handed it back to Frank. "Thanks for your help, let us know if you figure out more about the dirt."

"Of course I will officer. Mind if I ask how the case is going?" The entomologist got all excited waiting for the officers to answer him.

"We have a few leads we're looking into, nothing solid yet." Andrews answered walking out of the lab and then turning back, "honestly I'm not so sure this guy even knows what he's doing. He's probably just a troubled man with a damaged past and lots of screws loose in his head."

"He seems smarter than you are giving him credit for Detective. You might want to be careful or you could upset him." Frank watched after the officers and then went back to creating slides.

Back at their desks Andrews was still trying to shake the bad vibes from before. Best way she knew to do that was distract herself. "Geoff you hungry? How 'bout we grab some lunch?"

"Got an idea about where you'd like to go?" Geoff knew that look he was getting. Normally the look meant ice cream, and he prepared himself for Andrews to say Dairy Queen or Cold Stone.

She thought about it for a moment and then suggested, "Meat, I want meat!"

Geoff laughed at his partner. He definitely was not expecting that. The detective continued laughing as his phone rang and he picked up. "Baker... yes, I understand, we'll be right there." He turned to Andrews, "might want to ignore your stomach for a little."

"Oh really, and why is that exactly?" She thought better of her question immediately after she asked.

Baker grabbed his keys and headed toward the door. "Andrews, I'll fill you in when we get to the car."

They both walked out to the squad car. Geoff looked over at Andrews as he started the engine. "There was a body found at one of the local retirement homes." He paused to pull out of the station, "The officer on scene thinks this murder could be connected to our case."

It wasn't a long drive to the retirement home. A long line of flags outlined the drive, right after a big sign that read Montgomery Park Retirement Home. There were already numerous other police cars lined up by the side of the building. Crime scene tape mapped out an area and there was a mob of elderly people with their walkers and wheelchairs right by the tape. The medical examiner van was already here as well, so Andrews immediately started looking for Norm. He'd be the first person they would want to talk to.

Stepping out of the car Andrews could smell a mix of garbage and decaying flesh. Baker wrinkled his nose at the smell too, reaching into his pocket and grabbed nose plugs. Andrews just shook her head and pulled out her gun. She took out the clip and removed two bullets before placing them in her nose and putting her gun back together.

"What in the world are you doing Andrews?" Baker wasn't really surprised by her action but he was in disbelief that someone would shove bullets up their nostrils just to stop a smell.

Adjusting the bullets, she rolled her eyes at him, "They fit perfectly and block the smell. Plus this way if I run out of ammo I know where I have two more shots!"

Walking toward the crime tape, Andrews prepared herself mentally for what she would find. Already it appeared as though the body were in some sort of garbage compactor. Baker and Andrews looked at each other and gave questioning looks. Norm stepped out from behind the machine smiling widely that was never a good sign. The messier something was the happier Norm was, he liked a challenge.

"Hey guys, over here. Welcome to what could be the most disgusting thing you've ever seen. Looks like he was brutally stabbed and then thrown in here and crushed, because of that though, I won't be able to get you a positive id, till we get the dental back. He's in pretty bad shape." Norm stated, dressed in a blue jumpsuit and bits of food hanging off of him.

"Thanks Norm." Baker wasn't too excited to go look for himself, but it had to be done.

Andrews followed her partner towards the compactor. Trash and random food items covered the ground below and bags were ripped open everywhere. She thought she saw a finger and had to close her eyes to keep from contaminating the crime scene. Peering inside, Andrews didn't bother to hold back a gasp. The bottom was layered in boxes and cardboard. Above that was a mix of garbage bags torn apart and reddened masses of flesh. There appeared to be no way to distinguish between the victim's arms and legs. He was completely unrecognizable.

Lying in the corner of the area, Andrews made out to be what she thought was hair. Careful not to fall in, she leaned forward to get a closer look. A forehead became visible, matted in a dried bubbling substance. The victim's hair tangled in knots was lying across what was left of his face. Andrews noted the bite marks present on the victim. She assumed rats had made a feast of him, for his eyes were missing and scratch marks outlined his orbital eye sockets. Nothing else was visible without moving the victim's hair. The neck was indistinguishable from the trash pile that surrounded it.

"Worm really did a number on you poor old man." Baker had joined Andrews. He leaned over the edge of the compactor, pushing bags aside.

"Baker some parts I can't even tell what they are. This compactor completely destroyed this man's body." Andrews was becoming physically ill from the scene.

Her partner stepped back and waved over the CI crew. "Don't worry Andrews they'll go through it, you don't have to."

The two detectives left the scut team to do their work. Behind the crime scene lines, the residents of the complex were lining up to watch what was going on. There was a cluster of officers around two middle-aged men taking down notes. Baker headed off in that direction with Andrews tailing him.

"I think this could be the managers of the complex. I want to talk to them myself." He said over his shoulder.

As they got closer to the grouping, the officers looked up and scattered when they saw the detectives. The taller man who appeared to be more aged than the other reached out his hand first, "Hello, we just talked to those officers but if you need something more we'd be happy to tell you."

"And you are?" Baker questioned the forward man.

First pointing to himself, "I'm Carey Stevens the manager here" and then to the man slightly behind him, "and this is Doug Moore the co-manager here."

Andrews looked around and saw more residents coming out of back doors, she assumed led to their apartment. "This is a nursing home? How exactly does this place work?"

Carey looked at the detective and explained, "This is an independent retirement home. The residents are free to come and go as they please. We believe the man you found is Charlie Grayson, he seems to be the only one we wives couldn't find."

"Your wives work here too?" Baker asked the man.

"Yes, this is a job for couples, our wives went around and took note of who was in their rooms and who they knew would be out tonight. Charlie is the only one missing and we know he wouldn't have gone anywhere, he never left the building." Carey shook his head.

Doug spoke up, "We all liked Charlie, and he was a quiet guy. Pretty much kept to himself, never late for meals and was always at bingo Sunday nights. He's eighty-one, still moves around on his own. He didn't have a cane or a walker, the only people that visited him were his daughter and her husband the Wayne's."

"Did he ever get into arguments with other residents or did he have any enemies here that you know of? Anything that might help us?" Andrews had been jotting down all this information and was now trying to fill in the blanks that the managers hadn't helped with yet.

The two managers looked at each other and then into the crowd. Carey nodded to his left, "See that gentleman over there with the sweater vest on leaning on his walker with the thick black glasses? That's Daniel Jenkins, he and Charlie would get into fights a lot. We don't really know what over it was mostly done in the hallways away from other people. The other night, though Daniel came to dinner with a scratch near his eye, he claimed it was from Charlie."

"Like we told you, Charlie pretty much kept to himself. I do know though that his son-in-law was trying to get him to move into a home and that was a big battle between the families. Charlie has a bit of money from what I understand and the son-in-law seems after it, but he can't touch any of it till Charlie passed."

Baker was still watching the resident who the managers claimed to be at odds with the deceased. "Is there anyone that might have come into contact with the compactor tonight? Who normally is in charge of the trash around here?"

"That would be Joseph Zcap our dishwasher. He was on duty tonight and he was the one that called the cops, he's over there sitting in the squad car. The guy is a little eccentric, but he wouldn't hurt anyone." Doug pointed to an open car with a man sitting inside hunched over and holding his head.

"Thank you gentleman, I believe that's all we need for now. Please give your business card to one of the other officers in case we need to get a hold of you again." Baker shook the men's hands, Andrews following behind him.

The two detectives walked away from the managers toward the edge of the scene. "So what do you think?" Baker tilted his head in Andrews' direction.

"I think I wouldn't let my grandmother stay here, that's for sure. That man didn't have any friends it sounds like, he just kept to himself. That's not exactly how I would want to live out the rest of my life, along with only a son-in-law waiting for me to die so he could have my money." Andrews felt bad for the guy. She didn't have the slightest clue who wanted to off this guy though, it didn't seem like Worm's type of victim.

"I'm not so sure this is connected to our case, there seem to be things missing."

Andrews smirked, "I was just thinking that."

He sighed, "Well, think about it, the range in victim ages just grew quite a bit. This murder was a lot more brutal than any of the others, and where was the earthworm? Granted, there is a lot of the techs to sort through in that dumpster, but before it's always been at least a little obvious, especially with the Frankie girl. She was holding the worm when we found her."

"Geoff, I don't mean to be gross, but I'm really hungry and I still really want meat, can we please go to Bill Gray's and grab a burger or something?" Andrews pleaded with her eyes.

"You are a strange, strange girl. You just saw a man ripped apart by a garbage compactor and you're hungry?" He laughed at her, "Yeah, okay, let's go get you some meat!"

They drove to Bill Grays and we're excited to see their favorite waiter ready and waiting for them. Moment Rob says them coming he screamed and order back to the kitchen and pulled some cups onto the counter. "The usual, detectives?"

"Of course Rob, though can I have some extra curly fries please? We just got off a call and I haven't had anything to eat all day!" Andrews thanked the guy and took her cup over to the soda fountain.

Both detectives got their drinks and then waited for their numbers to be called. Going to the usual table they sat and for a while just ate in silence. Andrews finished off her burger and then picked at the fries while staring off into space. "How many other people do you think are already dead and we just haven't found them?"

"Well, isn't this just an exciting conversation to be having over burgers? I couldn't really tell you Andrews, guess eventually we'll find out." Baker kept eating.

"Seriously Geoff, don't you ever wonder about possible bodies lying in some ditch that no one will come across. They just decay and disappear into the soil? Leah and Frankie were pretty much out in the open, but now there's Charlie and he was in a trash compactor. If someone had done a better job at using the machine, no one would have ever known he was there. So what if Worm is just getting better at killing and hiding his victims?"

Baker knew where Andrews was going with this, "You mean like what if the girls were his first and it was more like practice to see what all he could do and get away with?"

Andrews nodded, "Yeah. I still say we could be going about this all wrong. It feels like there's more to the earthworms than we think and you saw how high that compactor was and if Charlie looked like all those other residents, I kind of think it took two people to get him into the compactor."

"You may be right, once they clean up the scene we'll have someone go out and practice with the dummy, see what is possible." Baker finished up his meal and sat there waiting for his partner to either finish her or to bring up another idea. He could tell from the wrinkle on her forehead that she was deep in thought.

"Tell you what Bethany, why don't we head back to the station and split for the night. You can go and talk Bailey and then get back to me in the morning with what you figure out." He snickered, "I know bouncing ideas off me works for you and all but I also know that bouncing them off your lab works even better."

"Geoff it's not even four yet, you sure you want to quit out this early?" Bethany was confused.

Again Geoff snickered at his partner, "I didn't say we're cutting out this early, whatever that phrase may mean. I'm telling you to go home and talk to your dog. I will go back to the station and do some paperwork and I will also make sure you have a tail home too, I know how you love having Perez around."

"You're hilarious. Okay, it sounds like a plan, let's head back to the station."

They both stood and waved to Rob as they left. The drive back was quiet, Bee has been already deep in thought about the case. Reaching the station the detectives said their goodbyes, Geoff headed into the station and Bethany for her car. She didn't even have time to put the key in the ignition before Perez came out of the station and got into his own car ready to follow her home. Bethany just shook her head, she was so ready to be lost of her protection, and in her mind it wasn't even necessary anymore.

When she reached home, Bee, fed Bailey and then grabbed a stack of Post-it notes and sat down with her white board to start thinking. "Perez goes to help yourself to the TV, I'm going to hang out in the dining room here."

"Alright Andrews, I'll just be over here watching some SpongeBob Square pants then." Perez headed for the couch and sat down to watch some cartoons.

Bethany just laughed at him, a grown man watching children's cartoons, typical. "Okay Bailey let's do this." She spread out the different colors and wrote at the top of each different color. Suspects, Victims, Locations, Evidence, Leads and Questions. On Suspects she wrote Jason Banner and Karl Montgomery. She thought Dr. Montgomery was really the only suspect they had but Jason was Frankie's boyfriend it was necessary to put him down just in case. The issue was neither men really fit into the latest murder. What connection did they have to, Charlie?

Setting that set aside, she picked up the victims stack and wrote down Leah Kummer, Frankie Gerald, and Charlie Grayson. Having three victims meant Worm could definitely be classified as a serial killer now, just what the Buffalo area needed. The first two victims had many things in common, but Charlie stuck out. Bee decided to just finish writing everything out and then she would try and piece it together. For Locations she just had Franklin and Mohawk, the UB North Campus and Montgomery Park retirement home. There were no leads currently and evidence was nothing but the earthworms found in the girls' throats and stomach contents. For Questions, there she filled up the Post-it note. Why the worms? Does the nursery rhyme have anything to do with it? Why the choice of victims and range in ages? What would the motive be? Just one person or multiple murderers? Is there even a pattern?

For an hour, Bethany went over what she had written down. She grabbed a map and tried to work out a pattern through locations, nothing. She tried to find a connection in the background between the girls and Charlie, nothing. There was nothing, they had no leads, nothing to go on. Tomorrow they could talk to Charlie's family and the dishwasher from the retirement home, but who knew if that would help or harm the situation. Sadly, it was like they had to wait for someone else to die to find something that might be the least bit helpful in solving this case.

Perez stood, "I'm going to run across the street quick and check in with the guys. You are going to be okay?"

"Yeah, no problem, go ahead. I know not to talk to strangers." She smiled at him.

Perez left the apartment and Bee went back to studying her notes. Bee heard a knock on the door and looked expectantly at Bailey. "You are going to get that or do I actually have to get up?"

The lab lifted her head to look toward the door. Bailey glanced at her master before putting her head back down. Bethany chuckled at her companion, pushing the dog off her lap. She stood announcing that she was coming and mumbling under her breath about them learning patience.

"I'm coming, you can really stop knocking now." Bethany opened the door, gasping in shock. "You." She barely got out before being interrupted.

"What are you thinking just opening the door like that and not even checking to see who's there first?!" The man growled at her, pushing by her and going inside. He looked each way down the hall before closing the door and locking.

Bethany grabbed at the Bailey's collar trying to stop her dog from attacking the intruder. "What are you doing here Kevin?"

Her visitor brushed his hair back with his fingers and worriedly watched her. "Aren't you going to say hi first before you start yelling at me?"

"I'm not going to yell at you, I just want to know what you're doing in my apartment." Bee tried her best not to look at him directly. She was a sucker for his stormy gray eyes.

Kevin sighed, "I'm in Buffalo because of Leah. I was worried about you. This isn't like one of your cases back home Bumble Bee, this guy is really dangerous."

"Don't talk to me like that. I'm not your Bumble Bee anymore. Thanks for your concern, but I can handle myself. Been doing it for months." She let go of the dog's collar and walked into the kitchen.

Bethany grabbed a glass from the cabinet and poured herself a glass of wine. Quickly drinking the first glass she passed another and then spun to face the man she had plans to marry once upon a time. That felt like a lifetime ago. Her reality was slipping from grasp and she knew he wasn't going to leave till she explained everything. He was the most stubborn person she knew, and that he was looking at her as though nothing had happened.

"What are you really doing here Kevin? If you just wanted to check on me, you could have just called." Bee took a sip of wine anxiously waiting for an answer.

Her ex-fiancé took a step toward her and pulled the wine glass from her hand. He placed it on the counter behind her, "You're a terrible drunk, don't drink because of me. I'm not worth that." Kevin reached up and held her face in his hands, "I never gave up on you. I'm here because I love you. I don't need to know why you ran, I just don't want to be shut out of your life again."

"I loathe when you do that." She fell into him and let herself melt in his arms.

Bailey's anxious barking broke the moment, and the two tore apart. "How about I make you some food and while I do that you can tell me what's going on." The gentleman proposed.

Bee looked at the clock and then back at Kevin. "I have a better idea. What if we took Bailey for a walk and I answered any questions you might have. Then afterwards, we can go to Elmo's it's a small bar off the highway."

Kevin leaned in to kiss her but was stopped by Bethany's hand. He instead held out his own hand, "Alright, so it will take some time to get to that point, but we will get back to it."

Bethany just laughed at him, and walked over to the closet. Her dog followed at her heels, knowing what the closet contained and that she would soon be getting attention. After hooking Bailey to the leash, Bee handed the dog off to Kevin and put on her coat.

"That felt naturally didn't it?" He smiled at her, raising his eyebrows in enjoyment at the look on her face. "We always said we wanted a dog."

Holding the front door open, Bethany ushered the other two out. "We said a lot of things Kevin, and Bailey is my dog."

Kevin held onto Bailey's leash when Bee tried taking it from him. "You said you would answer my questions, and I expect the truth from you Bethany."

"Go ahead, question away. I promise only to tell you the truth."

"This was because of that last job you did? The boy's brother is the one that made you run?" Kevin's smile fell and his face showed signs of being worried again.

Bee looked at the ground, "yes, it was because of Corey I had to leave. Naturally he blamed me for his brother's death and somehow from within jail he put a hit out on me." She paused just slightly to catch her breath. "My uncle thought it would be best to send me here. Only he and my boss here knew, well my partner does too now. Sky does as well, not everything but enough."

"Do you love me yet?" He stopped walking and turned to face Bee.

"I never stopped, and I never will. You and I are a match, as much as I hate to say that, we fit. I fit perfectly under your chin."

"Funny how that's what you chose to mention," he winked at her before continuing to walk.

They circled a tree a few blocks down and then started making their way back. About half way, Kevin reached and took the Bethany's hand. She only looked down and then went back to observe those around them. The two walked in silence till they got to the front door.

"Kevin, would you like to come in? I have the case files out if you want to help?" Bethany unhooked Bailey and let her go into the apartment.

"Always playing Ned and helping out Nancy Drew," he teased, "you of course will get all the credit in the end."

Bee playfully glared at him, "Oh, you like pretending you're a detective!"

The two sat in front of the couch on the floor. Bethany had brought over the wine from before and an extra glass for Kevin. He poured himself some and they picked up the first crime scene photos.

"Oh, how stupid of me! You shouldn't be helping, Leah was your cousin."

"Hey, hey, hey!" he cooed trying to calm Bee before she reached hysterics. "I can handle this, just let me help. Please Bethany."

She was sure this was a bad idea but she nodded yes to him anyways. Bee grabbed what was in his hand and lined up all the photos in order. Taking sticky notes she labeled each section with a day and time, the murders had taken place. She then grabbed the bag of gummy worms from earlier and placed on one each diagram she made of the victim's bodies. Bethany wasn't sure how much Kevin knew about the case, but she really hoped he'd spark at least a new idea.

"You always were organized and a little crazy with the sticky notes," jokingly he laughed but really he was rather impressed by her. Watching her think out cases was always a turn on for him, he loved a woman with a brain.

Bee again glared at him, it was a common gesture most of the time made out of love. "Do you want me to run everything by you or do you think you got it."

"Do your thing Sweetie, you know it makes me randy to watch you work!" The last part was said with a lisp as he leaned in closer to whisper it to her.

"You really do have issues, still fifteen at heart I see."

"Oh you love it! Seriously though, run me through the case." Kevin straightened up and focused on the pictures and notes in front of him.

Bee began to tell him about the case when Perez walked back into the apartment. "Seriously Andrews what did I tell you about not letting anyone in?"

"Technically Perez you didn't say to not let anyone in, just so you know." Bee shrugged. "This is Kevin, he's an old friend from back home. He's harmless basically."

The guys shook hands. "So are you staying or what is going on?" Perez was still wary about letting the man stay there. If the captain heard about this he could be demoted in an instant.

"Yeah he is, I can't get him to leave. So what did the guys downstairs have to say?"

"It's been a quiet night, you should be okay for now. We'll see how the night goes." Perez walked back over to the couch and started watching TV again.

Bee didn't give up for a few more hours. In that time, Kevin gave up trying to help and went to watch cartoons with Perez. Both guys had eaten dinner and tried to convince Bethany to take a break with no avail. Finally around ten that night, Kevin pulled a sleeping Bee away from the files and notes she had made and carried her to bed. He tucked her in and then returned to the dining room to clean things up. He saw the note she made about her letters suggesting someone check out the florist to see who was sending her the black roses with the death threats. Kevin decided he would do that tomorrow while she was at the station. He pocketed that note, said good night to Perez and headed back into the bedroom to sleep on the floor by the door. Kevin may not be able to do much to protect his girl but this made him feel like he was doing something important. Now that he finally found her and had her back, he wasn't about to lose her to some psychopath.

Chapter 6: Trout Worm

Bethany woke up the next morning feeling rested and ready to get back to work. She sat up in bed and laughed at her boyfriend on the floor snuggling with Bailey. What a pair those two made. Grabbing a pillow she threw it at Kevin, "Wake up and go make me some coffee mister!"

"Good morning to you too sweetie! Would you like any breakfast with that coffee, your highness?" Kevin just laughed and left for the kitchen after receiving a glare for an answer. "She sure is bossy, isn't she Bailey. I'll get you breakfast too puppy."

It was Sunday, not a bunch of officers would be at the station on duty today, which Bee saw as an opportunity to get more done at work with the computers to do some background checks and research capabilities. While enjoying her cup of coffee and watching cartoons with the guys, Bethany's phone rang. "Hey Geoff I was just thinking about giving you a call", she paused, "Yeah, I can definitely be there. Okay set them up, I'll be in shortly."

"What did he want?" Kevin questioned her.

"He scheduled some of the interviews related to the Grayson case for this morning, Geoff is requesting my presence so it looks like I got to go." Bethany ran around getting dressed and putting her notes together in her bag. She petted Bailey for a moment or so, kissed Kevin goodbye and then headed out the door. Two seconds later she poked her head back in, "Perez, I hate to break you away from your cartoons, but if I don't show up to the station with you attached my head is going to be on a platter with the captain so would you please come with? Thanks, you're a doll."

Bethany drove to the station with Perez following behind her in his car. As assumed the parking lot was empty as they drove in, crimes normally didn't happen on Sundays, which made it unnecessary to have the entire squad getting paid to sit around and do nothing. Walking in, Andrews was stopped at the front desk and handed a letter with a black rose. She pulled out a tissue from her purse and took the rose from the receptionist. Once she got to her desk, she called another officer over and handed him the rose asking him to take it to the lab to check for fingerprints. She quickly jotted down, then what the note had said, "Today my dear, I will come for you."

"Hey Andrews, saw you already got your rose for the day. Any good notes come along with it?" Baker stood in front of her desk, two coffees in hand. He reached out to give her, her and looked down at what she had just written. "Uh oh, let's go see the captain."

Andrews felt her phone going off in her pocket and looked down to check the caller ID, it was Skylar for the third time already this morning. Looking back up, she scolded her partner, "Now just wait a minute. Let's do the interviews first and then we can tell him. If we tell Harris now he's going to send me home and that's not okay with me, I want to be here to interview those people with you."

"Do you promise me you'll go home after we finish the interviews and talk to Harris?" Baker stared his partner down.

She raised her right hand, "I promise to go straight home after we finish the interviews and tell the captain about the note."

"Alright then, let's get to interrogate, all three are already here and ready for us." Baker started off down the hallway.

Before heading into the room, Baker opened up the file he was carrying and showed Andrews that first they were going to talk to Daniel Jenkins the man the managers had informed them fought occasionally with their victim. He mouthed ready to his partner and at her nod, he reached for the handle and opened the door. "Good morning Mr. Jenkins, how is your morning going?"

"Considering I've spent the last hour alone in this room, I would say it's going pretty shotty."

The older man was the stereotypical grouchy piece of work Baker thought he would be. "Well, I will make sure to make this quick so you can get out of here and back to your usual routine. I just have a few questions for you Mr. Jenkins."

"Why don't you start asking, I don't want to be late for lunch all the good salads will be taken." The man growled at Baker.

Both detectives looked at each other and shook their heads at how this man thought getting a good salad was more important than solving a murder. Baker opened up his file, "Mr. Jenkins how well did you know the victim Charlie Grayson?"

He grumbled, "As well as you'd know anyone locked up in a place where you have to see the same people every day. What does he have to do with me? I didn't push him into the trash, I can't even walk on my own."

"Yes, sir, we can see that you have a walker. Can you please describe your relationship with Mr. Grayson though? Was it friendly, where you agitated with him?" He paused to look at the older man not flinching at all, "the managers have told us that you two would fight sometimes, and can you tell us what those were about?"

"Those managers know nothing, they only think they do. You shouldn't listen to them about anything, they don't care if we live or die as long as they get their money!" Very bitter, Daniel shook his head fiercely, "Sure Charlie and I fought, gave us something to do. It was never anything serious we just fought to prove we were alive and men."

"What do you mean that you were men?" Baker questioned.

Daniel pointed a finger at the detective, "See, you never have been on the front lines fighting in a war, that's when you feel alive," He point at his heart, "you feel something in here when the bombs are blowing up around you and you're getting shot at. Living in a place like that piece of junk you lose that, you lose every feeling you have and you just die slowly. We fought to stay alive, to continue feeling something, in here," he stated as he pounded his chest.

Baker made a note in the margin of the report and then thanked the man for coming in, "That's all we have for you right now, we'll let you get back so you don't miss lunch. Thank you for your time Mr. Jenkins and please don't hesitate to call if you ever need anything or think of something that might help us find who did this to your friend."

"I never said we were friends," the man said gruffly as he struggled to stand, reaching for his walker to support himself.

"My apologies, sir," Baker nodded at the man as he held the door open to him. Hailing down an officer, he requested they walk the man out.

Andrews peeled herself from the back wall, "He couldn't possibly have done it, Mr. Grayson kept that man alive and it seemed they gave each other something to look forward to." She laughed a little, "Sure was a spunky old guy, wasn't he? So who's next on your list?"

"The son-in-law, Carson Wayne." Baker barely had time to get the name out before there was a knock on the door and an officer escorted Mr. Wayne in. "Please take a seat, sir."

"I don't understand why I'm being questioned about my father-in-law's death. I didn't kill him, why am I here?" Mr. Wayne seemed very nervous and highly agitated about being asked to come to the station.

Baker scribbled "shh" on the paper in front of him and showed Andrews. "Sir, we don't think you are responsible for Mr. Grayson's death. We asked you to come down to the station to ask you about his life at the retirement home that is all. Answer a few questions for us and we'll have you on your way."

She kept a straight face while she listened to her partner do his job. Andrews had seen him lying to suspects before. Sometimes it was necessary in order to get the right answers to the questions you wanted. If you just outright asked someone if they murdered another person 9.7 times out of 10 you can guarantee they'll tell you that they're innocent. In order to get to the truth you need to dance around the lies and get them to slip up. Seance, Mr. Wayne has been nervous and that was obvious in his mannerisms, Baker should have a rather easy time getting him to just open up.

"Mr. Wayne how did your father-in-law like working at Montgomery Park? Did he seem happy to be there for you?" Baker started out with a simple enough question, but still saw the man clench his hands into fists.

"Charlie seemed to like it okay enough, he would complain about the food a lot, but that seemed to be a common complaint from all the residents. The managers switch a few times a year at these places and that would upset him too. He never really complained about it." Carson seemed upset by the statement he had just made.

Baker marked a few things down on the file and then asked another question, "Roughly how much money are you about to inherit because of Mr. Grayson's death?" He didn't need to look up from the files to know what Mr. Wayne's expression probably was.

"I... I don't know what you're trying to get to Detective but I did not have my father-in-law killed for his money!" Carson unclenched his hands and started shaking, "I didn't kill him. I didn't kill Charlie!"

"Sir, I'm going to ask you once to calm down. There is no need to become defensive if you didn't do anything wrong. I just wanted to know how your finances were going to look after this murder is shut and closed." Baker now looked up and waited for a reaction.

Carson calmed down fast and just stared at the detective, "What do you mean by that, shut and closed? I can't have my money until you find whoever killed the geezer?"

"Ah, how quickly you snap out of the act Mr. Wayne. Why don't we start over and you explain to me your relationship with the deceased." Baker leaned back and his chair and smiled smugly to Andrews.

She watched as the man tried to explain himself out of the lies he just got himself stuck in. Her partner was excellent in the interrogation room, she had learned a lot from him since first getting to Buffalo. Andrews felt her phone vibrate in her pocket again and checked to see that it was Skylar. Something was up but she didn't have time right now to find out just what her best friend wanted, it would have to wait.

Carson continued to try and dig himself out of the hole but was saved when there was a knock on the door. The detectives looked at each other wondering who would interrupt an interrogation like that. Baker stood and opened the door finding himself to be facing the captain. He stepped outside motioning Andrews to follow him.

"Andrews, when were you going to tell me that you got another rose and message this morning? You didn't think the threat of them coming for you today was important enough to tell me?" Captain Harris looked between the detectives.

Baker could clearly see how pissed the captain was and tried to help Andrews out a little, "I had made her a deal sir that she could help with the interrogations and then she was going straight home with a few officers for protection."

"Ah, so you two decided that you ranked high enough to make the call yourselves is that it? You think gambling with her life is okay to do without consulting me, the person put in charge to keep her safe by her uncle?" The captain put his hands on his hips and started to pace. "Baker you finish the interrogations, and try to hurry with the one you have there's a highly talkative man out in the waiting room who I believe is next and he's driving my officers crazy. I want him out of that waiting area as soon as possible." He then turned to Andrews, "You missy, you're coming with me back to my office so we can discuss what exactly to do with you."

"Yes sir," Andrews sighed, shrugging her shoulders at her partner. "Geoff call me later and fill me in please with the rest of the questionings."

"Will do, stay safe Bethany." Baker said before walking back into the interrogation room.

Andrews followed the captain back to his office and took a seat opposite him. Her phone yet again vibrated, this time she didn't even have to look to know it was Skylar calling again. The rose and note were on Harris' desk in a plastic bag. The flower already was beginning to wilt.

"This is becoming quite serious Andrews, you must realize that. Now I called your uncle and we've both agreed the safest place for you right now is your apartment. If the roses can get to the station then you can't be here." He moved some papers around and then read something before looking up again, "I'm assigned two officers to stay with you inside your apartment at all times and then there will be two unmarked cars outside of your complex. If you even try to leave your apartment or get away from your guards then I will put you on suspension and take you off the Worm case."

"Sir, that's not necessary. I will listen and stay put, but I don't see any risk, they've always been empty threats and it's probably just Corey's gang back home, that's all." Andrews pleaded with her boss, "This has nothing to do with the case I'm on, you can't take me off."

Captain Harris ran his fingers through his hair, "I understand your frustration Andrews but my first priority is keeping you safe, if that means taking you off the case and locking you in your apartment till we catch whoever is sending you these roses that's what I'm going to do."

"What if I make a deal with you?" He was right, she was extremely frustrated and growing steadily tired of this whole ordeal, "What if after tonight I'm still alive and everything is okay I can come back to the office and just stay here. I'm surrounded by officers with guns if something was going to happen don't you think I'd be safer here around all of you than in my apartment with only a few people protecting me?"

The captain thought about it for a while and then sighed heavily, "Alright Andrews you have a deal. Cooperate tonight and if nothing goes down then you can come back tomorrow and continue working on the case, if anything and I mean anything more happens though and I tell you to go home, you do it immediately and you do not fight with me. Understand?"

"Yes sir." She was glad she got him to compromise a little, she hated the idea of being locked up like a criminal on house arrest. "And sir, if something does go down again, I would like you to help me get in touch with the D.A. and I'll take his deal."

"Are you sure you don't want to wait until that becomes necessary first and maybe talk to Baker about that first?" Harris questioned the detective's logic.

"I'm sure sir, this is what will be necessary if anymore happens and I don't want anyone else but us to know about it please." Andrews was stubborn and she had made up her mind a few days ago about taking Topher's offer to be the bait. She knew though that if it ever came up, not only Baker but Kevin would throw a fit and that was something she could afford to let happen. They would probably get in the way and ruin everything.

The captain picked up the phone and dialed, "Yes Perez please come to my office and bring your partner with you."

Didn't take long for the two to reach the captain's office. "What's up captain?" Perez asked, "We back on babysitting duty?"

"Yes you both are, I want you boys to follow young Detective Andrews here home and stay with her until tomorrow. If anything is suspicious call me immediately. Don't let anyone else into the apartment either, there was another death threat sent today." The captain said sternly.

"Uh, captain if we tell that boyfriend of hers to stay away that could get ugly." Perez looked over at Andrews, "You know Kevin won't stay away."

"I promise he's harmless captain, and he won't get in the way of your protection detail, I'll make sure of it." She told her boss.

Captain Harris nodded, "Yes I've heard he's been hanging around a lot. Just make sure he stays out of the way and I don't care if he stays over. Don't let anyone else in that apartment though! Do we all understand each other?"

"Yes captain," they all said in unison.

"Good. You're all excused, get out of my office."

Detective Andrews and the other officers left the station and headed for their cars. Once they were all in, Perez drove over to where Andrews had parked and waved for her to go in front of him.

113

Andrews pulled out and felt her phone vibrate again in her pocket, she made a conscious decision to call Skylar back the moment she got home. Sky had never been this persistent before in calling, it must be important.

The officers arrived at the apartment and found Kevin already there and waiting with Bailey inside. "You're home early, what happened?" Kevin immediately went over to Bethany and held her in front of him waiting for an answer.

"Oh it was nothing really, I just got another rose from my admirer and a cute little message saying he was coming for me tonight." Andrews sarcastically told Kevin, trying to escape his grip.

Kevin didn't let her slip out of his grasp and looked past her to the officers, "Two?! They only sent two officers to protect you?"

"Look, hon" She started, "You need to chill and let me go, and you're starting to hurt my arm. These officers are more than capable of protecting me, and I'm able to protect myself as well. Plus this isn't it, there are two unmarked cars out front as well. I'm going to be okay."

He loosened his grip and let her go to great Bailey. "Okay so what are we all going to do tonight?"

Bethany looked up from her position on the floor with the dog to Perez and his partner, "You guys can help yourself to the TV, I have a phone call I need to make and then we can order pizza or dinner or something. I'll make a call to the guys below and ask them to run out for something and bring it up, since none of us are allowed to leave."

"Who do you need to call?" Kevin followed Bethany into her bedroom watching her pull out her cell phone.

"Sky's been trying to call me all day, I really need to call her back. Is that okay with you or is this against your rules or something?" Bethany stated heavy in sarcastic attitude.

"Sweetie you need to relax, you're stressed. Call Skylar and then you and I can play a game or something tonight and get your mind off the case and this crazy stalker."

"Thanks Kevin." She held the door open and motioned with her head for him to leave, this was a phone call she thought should be made in private. After he left she dialed her best friend's phone number.

"Hello?" The voice anxiously answered on the other end of the line.

"Hey Sky, what's up? I was at work, I couldn't answer your calls at all until now." Bethany explained.

Skylar squealed with excitement, "Bee I wanted you to be the first to know! I got in at a fashion show! I get to do my own line and show it for fashion week in New York City!"

"That's great Sky! I bet you already have a bunch of sketches done up, don't you?" Bee was excited for her friend. Razz Designs was something Skylar has been working on for years and it was good that she was finally getting her chance to get the designs out there to be noticed and recognized for her hard work.

"Yes I do! And, remember when I first started my company you promised you would model for me if I ever got a show other than the ones I put on myself? Well, Bee that time has come. Now I know you have this whole issue going on and you need to be in Buffalo and can't be in public or whatever it is but this isn't for a few more months yet." Sky took a breath and waited to see if her friend would make a comment, when nothing came, she continued, "I'm hoping you can close whatever case you're working on and work everything out so you can model for me. What do you think? It'd be in June, then you'll be able to model?"

Bee really wanted to tell her friend, yes, but she just couldn't make that kind of commitment without knowing how things were going to turn out. As things were going it could possibly take months to solve this case, she just didn't know. She ran the possibilities through her mind and tried to think up a way she could make her best friend happy and still deal with the case if that is what it came down to.

Her silence must have scared Sky because the begging began soon afterward, "Please say yes Bee, please!"

"Alright, alright! I will do my best to work things out so I can model for you. You just need to promise not to put me in anything too crazy, okay?" Bee knew what kind of outfits Sky was possible of making and didn't want there to be an issue at the station or any physical evidence of her in something either completely crazy or totally risqué. "Keep it classy Sky!"

"Yes ma'am! And thank you so much, you won't regret this Bee I promise!" Sky got quietly thinking about what she could make Bee wear for her show.

The two friends finished their conversation talking about life back home in Pennsylvania and the relationship blooming in Buffalo with Kevin and Bee. Once they hung up, Bee left her bedroom and returned to the living room to catch the guys watching a war movie on TV. Collectively they agreed on subs for dinner and called to the officers stationed outside to go fetch the food and bring it up to them. After dinner the four of them played scrabble and then the guys went back to watching TV and Bee went to lay down.

She must have been exhausted from the day's events because it didn't take long for her to fall asleep. The next morning she woke up to the smell of pancakes and bacon. Not even bothering to comb her hair or check how she looked in the mirror first, Bee stumbled into the kitchen and found Kevin making breakfast. Bee looked around and noticed the officers were missing and so was her dog.

"Kevin, where's Bailey?"

He turned and smiled at her appearance, even tasseled she looked cute in the morning. "Last night after you fell asleep, Perez took her for a walk and currently he's out with her again this morning. The other one, I don't know his name, he is out in the hall talking to the captain on the phone." Putting some food on a plate, Kevin held out the breakfast with Bee, "Would you like something to eat?"

"Yes, thank you." Bee took the plate from Kevin and sat down at the table.

Halfway through breakfast, Perez came back with Bailey. The puppy ran over to Bee and excitedly waited to be petted. "Hi buppy, and how's my baby?" Looking at Perez then, "How was she for you? Did she go?"

"She was fine, she's such a good walker. We walked around the block a few times and then jogged around once, that wore her out enough that she was ready to come back." Perez helped himself to some breakfast.

Perez's partner came back into the apartment and handed the phone off to Perez who had just sat down to eat. "Hey captain, yes, she's fine, want us to bring her back in?" Perez looked over at Andrews who was staring him down. "And what about the boyfriend?" He paused listening to the captain's instructions. "Yes sir, I will." Perez hung up and started eating the food in front of him.

"Are you kidding me? You're going to eat, you aren't going to tell me what that was all about! Perez!!" Bee smacked him on the shoulder. "Am I under house arrest a little longer or do I get to go back to the station?"

"Calm down Andrews, he said if you're alive that you're allowed to come in and you're supposed to bring the boyfriend with, he'll stay at the station tomorrow too." Perez looked over at Kevin, "Hope you didn't have anything important planned for today."

Kevin shook his head, "I am perfectly okay with going to the station, and I didn't have any intention of letting Bee out of my sight."

The group of them got ready and finished their breakfasts before heading out. Two unmarked cars were still parked in front of Bethany's apartment complex, the men inside, already drinking probably their second cups of coffee for the morning. A line of cars heads for the station, Andrews and Kevin in the lead followed closely by Perez and his partner and the undercovers bringing up the rear. Arriving at the station, Baker is waiting by the door with the captain slightly behind him.

"Well good morning to the both of you, didn't realize I needed an escort into the station now too." Andrews laughed at how over the top this was getting.

Baker's face was stern and worried, "Bethany for the past two hours, on the hour you have been receiving a black rose. It hasn't stopped."

"Well is there any notes with it or just roses?" Andrews couldn't say she was surprised, she never expected the flowers and roses just too suddenly stop.

"No, it's just flowers but we can't trace them, we don't know where they're coming from." He answered back.

"I may be able to help you with that a little." Kevin said.

All eyes were on him for the moment and the captain stepped forward, "I'm going to assume you're the boyfriend. Can we please continue this in my office, I don't want anything to be overheard in case this creep is already in the station and we just don't know it."

Andrews, Kevin and Baker followed the captain back to his office. Her protectors broke off and went to do their own work, babysitting detail was canceled for the time being. Upon reaching the office, Andrews and Kevin sat down with Baker standing by the door, angled so he could see if anyone was coming.

"Now, is it Kevin? Why don't you explain what you meant by being able to help." The captain leaned back in his car curious how the man could offer any help at all.

Kevin looked over at Andrews knowing he was going to be in trouble later, but it was all for her safety so hopefully she would understand that he couldn't just sit around and do nothing. "The other day I went to the only florist around here that I know sells black roses in singles. The guy working there told me there hadn't sold any recently, but they did sell black dye to dip roses in." He paused and looked around the room, "Maybe this guy is making them black himself instead of buying them and then he just gets someone to deliver them for him?"

The captain was silent for a while and then picked up his phone, "George I want you to test the roses and see if they were dyed by an amateur. I'll have someone send you dye to test it against." Hanging the phone up he turned to Kevin, "That was very stupid of you to get yourself involved but we appreciate the information. Baker and Andrews I want you to stay at the station today and check in with me regularly. Kevin I'm going to assume you aren't leaving so try not to get in the way and whatever you see or hear here needs to stay confidential. Do you understand?"

"Yes sir, I just want to help keep Bethany safe. That's all." He looked over at her worry creasing his forehead.

The two detectives and Kevin left the captain's office. Once at his desk, Baker sat down and laughed frustratingly at the rose waiting on his partner's desk. "This guy sure is persistent, that's for sure."

Andrews hailed over an officer and asked them to take the rose down to the lab, then she sat down at her own desk and motioned for Kevin to pull up a chair. "You never called me last night Baker, how did the rest of the interrogations go?"

"You didn't miss anything, Mr. Wayne just whined and cried about how his father-in-law hated him and didn't want him to have any money or be happy. That dishwasher guy then was beyond eccentric and he wouldn't shut up. The guy seemed to have a comment on everything and an opinion to follow." Baker chuckled remember how the interview had gone, "Most that guy could have done is talk Mr. Grayson to death but he's harmless."

"So we still have nothing then?" she sighed heavily and rubbed her forehead. "How are we expected to solve a case if there are no leads and so far there aren't any connections? Have you heard from Norm yet? Did the old man at least have worms as his last meal?"

"Yes actually, he did have worms in his stomach contents. Norm is still working on it though, apparently the guy was in more pieces than what Norm would have liked." Baker was glad he didn't have the job of putting poor Mr. Grayson back together again.

Kevin leaned over and looked at the pictures Andrews had on her desk. "Oh Kevin, you don't want to look at those, they're of your cousin. Trust me you really don't want to see any of these." Andrews pulled them away from him.

"Fine, so can I look at your board or will that bother me too?" Kevin hissed quietly so only Bethany could hear.

She turned and glared at him, "We can run over things and maybe something will come up that we can go with. Eventually a lead will come to light, all murderers slip up eventually."

An hour went by with them just having shuffled papers around and stared at the board a little. Junior stopped by interrupting the silence and handed Andrews a black rose. "This came for you a little while ago."

"Junior, I need you to take that straight down to the lab. Did you see who brought it in?" Baker was quick to question the rookie.

"No, I just saw it sitting on the front desk out there with a note that it was for Detective Andrews so I thought I would bring it to her." Junior looked worried. "Did I do something wrong?"

Baker rolled his eyes, damn rookies. "Did anyone else touch this rose other than you?"

"No?"

"Please take it down to the lab and make sure you let them take your fingerprints so they can eliminate them. Next time you see a black rose for Detective Andrews, don't touch it. Okay?" he sternly told the rookie, hoping something would sink in.

"Yes, sir." Junior pulled back his hand and walked down to the lab taking the rose with him.

Andrews watched the boy go, "I don't like him." She looked over at Baker, "Do you like him?" Not waiting for an answer she repeated herself, "I don't like him."

The pattern repeated itself for hours. Andrews grew tired of everything and after lunch she snapped. "I'll be back you two, Kevin just hang out here. I need to talk to the captain."

The guys watched her leave, Baker mumbled under his breath, "This can't be good."

"What do you mean by that? What can't be good? She's just going to talk to the captain isn't she?" Kevin was confused.

"Yeah, that's what she's doing. She's going to talk about the captain about signing her death certificate early. I knew this would push her to take Topher's deal, stupid girl." Baker just shook his head ignoring Kevin's rapid questions. "Look, when she gets back you ask her yourself, I'm staying out of this one."

"But she's your partner, how can you just stay out of it?" Kevin attempted to get him into telling him. He wasn't enjoying not knowing what was going on but it didn't sound like he would enjoy hearing the answers to his questions either.

Baker looked over at him, "You're right, she is. I'm not going to just watch her use herself as bait though, there are better ways to handle this." That's where the conversation ended, Baker refusing to say anything else.

Andrews knocked on Captain Harris' door. "Sir, mind if I come in?"

Without looking up from his desk, the captain scolded his detective. "You were supposed to check in a while ago. Did you forget?"

"No, sir. We just got caught up in the case. Sir, since we last talked I have continued to receive these roses. I think it's time we contacted Topher." Andrews waited to see what the captain's reaction would be. It's not like she hadn't warned him this is where her mind was going.

Knowing how stubborn his detective was he knew it was pointless to try and talk her out of it, "Andrews even if I call the D.A. you can always back out of this deal. No one is going to make you go through with this if you don't want to."

"I understand, sir."

"Alright, then I want you and me to discuss details first before we call Christopher. I want a plan.

Chapter 7: Red Wriggler

Andrews and Baker sat at their desks and put on a good show of doing nothing for what seemed like hours. When the phone rang on the Baker's desk and Andrews checked the clock it had only been a half hour since she returned from the captain's office. She watched her partner talk on the phone not hearing anything that was being said. Andrews jumped when she felt something glide across the top of her hand. She looked down and saw that Kevin had reached over, his hand now covering hers. She smiled back at him, sending a silent thank you.

"Alright, looks like Norm has done the best he can and would like us to head over there." Baker looked then at the couple still staring at each other, "I'd let you bring prince charming along but I don't think that's permissible."

"It's okay, Detective, I don't need to go with to see a dismembered body. If you don't mind, I'll hang out here till you guys get back." Kevin moved his hand and let Andrews stand up.

She leaned over and did something to her computer before joining Baker, turning back, she once again smiled at Kevin, "I put up that bubble game you like so much on the screen, knock yourself out while we're gone."

The detectives went to the morgue to meet Norm. The doors didn't have to open for them to already get a whiff of the decaying flesh inside. They were greeted by the medical examiner as they entered.

"Sorry about the smell, unfortunately there's nothing we can do about that. After many hours we finally have as many parts as I think we're going to be able to find and piece together. I'm actually waiting for a friend of mine to stop by and give a second opinion, but it looks to me as though this man was hit on his occipital lobe with a blunt object." Norm walked over to where the x-rays were posted on the wall.

He pointed to the first one, "here you can see that his occipital lobe was struck in two different locations. I believe this, on the right is the fatal one. Also," he paused to move to the next section, "It appears his right clavicle was broken and numerous ribs as well as his sternum. Over here it shows that his radius is shattered, the ulna is missing on the left forearm but he has his right yet. The thoracic vertebrae are all fractured, some of the lumbar are missing and the cervical are chipped."

"So basically there's not a bone in this man's body that wasn't injured in some way?" Baker knew part of what Norm was talking about, but some of the bones names went over his head, even with the x-rays to look out it was still hard to distinguish which bone went where and did what.

Norm nodded, "Yes, there was only a few hands and foot bones that survived the brutal murder."

"What about time of death?" Andrews looked up from the notes she had been taken, "Can you even determine what that is with his body being in this condition?"

"I will get back to you on that after my colleague shows up and we talk first. Right now though, and please do not quote me on this, I would have to say the man was hit on the head about an hour before he was thrown into the dumpster, when that occurred though I couldn't tell you yet." Norm looked at each x-ray again, "His body is too mutilated to say much of anything right now."

"An hour?" Andrews asked, "Can you tell if any of the other damage was done during that time?"

Norm shook his head, "It did seem like a long time to me as well, but as far as I can tell, the man was struck on the back of the head and then about an hour later, thrown into the compactor."

"It just seems odd for the time gap. I was simply curious." Andrews said.

Baker walked over to Norm's desk and picked up the case report Norm had started on their third

victim. "What about any evidence of earthworms? Did you really find them in the stomach contents?"

"Yes, there was some worm goop as I've come to call it. There were not any whole ones,

however in his throat or in his hand. The rest of what was in the compactor is still being searched

through, but I can let you know if any whole ones come up." Norm thought for a moment, "I'm not an

expert on worm murders but I would have to say that the mo. Is the same with this one as with the girls.

His last meal seems to have been earthworms."

"Lovely." Andrews spoke for the first time since being in the basement. "That means we really

do have a serial killer now that is completely random!"

Baker puts his hand on her shoulder, "Relax Andrews, eventually we will find him. Trust me it

always seems more doomed than anything right before a break comes in the case."

"Well, hopefully that comes before we have a pile up of victims."

"I second that", Norm jumped back in, "Last thing I need is a pile up of victims, this guy alone

took up a few of my tables, I'm running low as it is."

Both detectives laughed nervously, "We both hope no one else becomes victim to worm's evil

before we can catch him." Baker stated talking to his partner as well.

"Nor we should probably leave you to your work, it looks like you still have a lot of it." Andrews

peered around the morgue. Most of the autopsy tables were taken and there were notes on each one

labeling which part of the body the fragments came from. There was a table that looked like it had yet

to be cleaned and another which held the fragments that couldn't yet be placed somewhere. Andrews

would have never though a trash compactor could be so deadly, but then again till she became a detective there were many things she never thought could be a weapon and found it could not only kill someone but completely mutilate their bodies as well.

"Oh, there is something else I should probably tell you," Norm walked back over to the x-rays. "Right here is where the lingual artery is, on our vic here his was cut and it wasn't zig-zagged like the rest of him, this was cut with a smooth edge."

The detectives looked at each other. "What exactly does that mean Norm?" Baker questioned where the medical examiner was going with this bit of information. So what if the artery was cut, the man went through a garbage compactor.

"What I'm trying to tell you is that his artery, which leads to the tongue was cut with a pair of scissors. Someone with an extensive, medical background would have been able to find this eatery." He walked over then to his desk and grabbed a book off the shelf behind it. Flipping through some pages he found what he was looking for. "Here, see how small it is and how there are plenty of other arteries surrounding it. Sure, you could just look for the one that's leading toward the tongue, but it's never that easy once you finally pick through the facial surrounding the facial muscles."

"Okay, now that I understand can you please explain how this helps the investigation? What would cutting that artery do to a person?" Andrews was trying really hard to follow what Norm was saying, but she was a detective not a doctor, she had no idea what he was talking about and couldn't even begin to try and guess and appear to understand.

Norm shrugged and flipped through some more pages, "I honestly don't have any idea why your murderer would want that cat. At first I was thinking he wanted to kill this man slowly, but cutting that artery alone wouldn't do anything fatal enough. I then wondered if maybe he started the process but something or someone interrupted him so he opted for just bashing the guy on the back of the head."

"There's no way you can tell what was used to it, if it really was just a scissors or maybe something in the compactor sliced it?" Baker wanted to be sure this was something before they wasted time running with it. Then again, they currently didn't have any other leads, so where would the harm be in looking into it?

"Now there really isn't. I guess there could have been something in that compactor that could make that sort of cute, but I don't see what could have made a smooth cut. There are no striations or marks at the ends of the artery where it was cut. It shows no damage at all." Norm furled his brow, "I honestly don't understand it myself and I've been stuck on this for a while now. I plan on asking my colleague when he gets here."

The detectives moved toward the door, "Alright, well let us know if the two of you come up with anything else we should know or if there's any other information at all. Thanks for your help Norm!" Baker held the door open for Andrews as they walked out.

"This case just got a little stranger." Andrews was very confused.

Baker laughed at his partner, "Yes, sometimes they do that. Do you need to check on your sweetheart or is it okay if we stop by the lab on the way back to check on those roses and see if they found anything involving the dye?"

"I'm not his mother, I'm sure Kevin is fine. He's addicted to that computer game so I'm pretty sure he's content in just trying to beat his last score. We can head over to the lab, I'm curious myself as to if they found anything or not."

They walked over to the lab and found one of the technicians working on the roses in the back. Andrews gasped when she saw how full the box was sitting next to the workstation. It seemed she had received a few more roses than people had told her. She wasn't sure if that made her happy that people were protecting her or if she had issues feeling like a child being protected like that. She did have the right to know, didn't she?

"My aren't we popular." Baker commented to Andrews seeing the box too. "Makes you feel like it's Valentine's Day in a Tim Burton movie and you're the most popular girl in school."

"I don't think that's something I should be proud of Baker. Those roses look like they're fit for a funeral." Andrews was not enjoying the attention or the thought of what those roses meant.

She knew she was hiding it well but fear was creeping up on her and it was becoming harder to fake not caring about the notes or the roses. Soon, though she would be calling Topher and becoming bait to catch Corey and his goons. She did have the thought before, though, wondering if it even was Corey, who was sending her those notes. There was the possibility out there that it could be someone in connection with the case or even just a stalker. Those weren't completely uncommon as people thought. A lot of times when cases became public and were on the media stations a lot, some nutter out there would grow fascinated with those involved in the case and become stalkers, or completely obsessed to a fatal degree. That's when having a job that was sometimes in the spotlight became dangerous. Normally it was the celebrities or people of "rich status" that found themselves victims to these sorts of situations, but it was known to be possible for those in the police department as well.

"If you've zoned out, how bout we go find out what they've discovered about your gifts." Baker gave his partner a little push toward the work table. "Trey, how's it going? Do you have anything to tell us about those flowers you've been looking at all morning?"

"Well, if it isn't Detective Baker and Detective Andrews. It's rare that we see any of you down here, normally you send your little workers to fetch us your things." Trey grabbed his notebook and held it out so the detectives could see. "I took your roses Andrews and had them tested and analyzed. They were definitely all dyed in the same manner and with the same medium. It was in fact that dye the officers brought to me from the floral shop."

Andrews grew excited, "So you found out, then that this guy really did buy the dye from the florist by my apartment complex?"

"Yes, I can easily confirm that. I can also tell you that each rose is missing a petal. At first I thought it was just lost during delivery, which happens sometimes. Messengers aren't always as careful as they should be with things that are so fragile. When I looked closer though," Trey spun his chair over to a stack of pictures taken of the flowers, "I found that each rose had an empty area by the stem where a petal should have been connected."

"Is it possible that's where the guy held the flower while he was dyeing it? I don't understand what the point would be to pulling off a petal." Andrews went from being excited back to confused and feeling hopeless.

Trey shook his head, "No, you hold the flower by the stem when you dye it because you want the entire head to become saturated with the dye. I think maybe he's saving those petals for something in particular, or maybe he messed up and touched a part of the flower knowing he left a fingerprint and instead just decided to pull that petal off rather than risk being found out."

"That wouldn't explain why they're all missing just one petal though," Baker noted.

"True, I didn't say I had all the answers for you, I'm just telling you what I discovered. What you do with that information is up to you I can't really help you any more than what I already have." Trey put down the pictures and his notebook.

Baker asked a copy of Trey's notes and findings be sent back upstairs, and then both detectives excused themselves and headed for their desks. As Andrews guess, Kevin was still sitting there playing on her computer. As they got closer she could tell though that he had changed from playing the bubble game to researching something on the internet.

"Kevin, what are you doing?" Andrews saw him jump and quickly minimize the window.

Standing up and moving back to the chair by the side Kevin pecked Andrews on the cheek before sitting back down. "I'm not doing anything, why would you think I'm doing something?" He didn't allow her time to respond, "So how did it go at the morgue? Did you find anything helpful out?"

"Norm said there's still some work to be done on the body but from what he knew now we found the earthworm connection with this victim as well. There was also a lot of damage to the skeleton of our victim, he took quite the beating." Baker answered for Andrews.

She continued, though, "There was something about the tongue too, but then in the lab. Trey told us that the flowers were dyed and they were from that store by my apartment. He also said there was a petal missing from each of the flowers, could just be a coincidence or related to the case. The answer is unknown right now." Andrews sat down at her desk and pulled up the computer's history. "That's basically all you missed."

"Sweetie, what are you doing?" Kevin watched what Andrews was doing with the computer and knew she wouldn't find anything, he had cleared the history but wished she would just trust him and not feel the need to search.

Andrews frustrated at not finding anything, glared at her boyfriend and went to straighten up her desk. Captain Harris came over to the detectives, he glanced once at Kevin and then turned his back ignoring him while focusing on his officers. "You two have anything you need to tell me?"

"No?" Baker was trying to think of something the captain would want to know but was stumped.

Looking just at Detective Andrews the captain raised his eyebrows, "You forgot to mention how popular you've been all day. I had the guys at the front keep a tally on your flowers." He paused for a moment trying to read her face, "You got forty-five black roses today Bethany. Did you know that?"

"Sir, Baker and I were at the lab a little while ago and I saw the box but I didn't count them."

"You need to go home detective, I thought maybe the station would be the safest place for you but apparently I was wrong." The captain scratched his head, "I'm really not sure what to do with you Andrews."

Andrews opened the drawer and grabbed her keys. "I'll go home and you can send the babysitters along. What we discussed earlier though is still on sir, I hope you take care of that for me."

"Of course, please stay safe. Right now I think I fear your uncle more than this serial killer." Harris laughed nervously, "Who knew a young thing like you could be so much trouble?"

Kevin spoke up, "Oh trust me sir, and she can be a handful more than you know."

Andrews slugged Kevin. "You would say that in front of my boss."

"The truth? Sure, I wouldn't lie to the man!" he chuckled at her frustration.

"Alright, alright pack up your stuff and get on home. I'll call you in the morning and we'll talk about what to do next. Stay safe." The captain said his final word of caution and then walked back to his office.

"Actually, do you mind if I stay and watch Baker's press release?" Andrews looked at her partner, "he really could use the support," she teased.

"Thank but I'll be fine," Baker replied pushing Andrews down the hall. "Go home and eat some ice cream. "

"You would go there. Don't mess up!" She said before finally starting to leave.

She said goodbye to her partner and then started for the front door. The entire walk through the station made her feel like she was in a fishbowl, everyone was staring at her as she passed. Andrews wasn't sure if she was being judged by her fellow officers or what the looks were for.

On the way back to the apartment Andrews talked Kevin into stopping for coffee at Tim Horton's. The officers already trailing her stopped and got some coffee and donuts as well before they all headed back to Andrews' apartment. Yet another fun night of hiding out and getting nothing done, all against her will. She wondered what would happen if she just took off and did her own thing. Where would she even go? Probably home to solve that issue, in case they ended up being related. For now back to reality being trapped in her apartment.

Reaching the front door of the complex, the manager came running out to catch the officers. "Miss Andrews!! Miss Andrews, there was a package for you a little while ago. I tried to reach you at the station but they said you had gone home. I didn't know how else to get a hold of you."

"It's okay Margie, where's the package?" Andrews looked behind her making sure Perez and the rest of her escorts were following before going inside to claim the package. She didn't need to open anything, just walking in the front door it was obvious who the sender was and what they had sent. "Perez, please bag that jar and get it back to the station immediately."

The officer went over and picked up the jar of worms sitting on the front desk using a napkin from the donut he had finished in the car. "Andrews, it's not a good sign that Worm knows where you live." He stopped talking when she sent him a look of death. "I'm just saying Andrews, a jar of worms at your apartment building isn't a good sign, that's all."

"Perez, get that to the lab now!" She turned to her landlady, "Margie, who delivered this to you?"

Margie shook with fear, "I don't know, it was just the normal postal man that has always____ delivered here. This is bad isn't it? I don't need any trouble here Miss Andrews, I have grandchildren and cats that need me."

"No harm will come to you, this was for me." Andrews turned to the officers behind her, "I want a couple of you stationed down here to keep Margie safe. I want a car out front at all times and then when Perez gets back sent him up for me please." She grabbed Kevin by the arm and started walking toward the elevator, "You're with me and you're staying over again tonight, no leaving."

Once inside the elevator, Kevin pulled Andrews to him, "Look at you being all controlling and fiery," he leaned closer to her, "I like it."

Andrews pushed him away, "My life is in danger, Worm now knows where I live and you're being turned on by me giving orders? You do realize that I'm the detective here, I am above them in rank."

Kevin sighed, "Yes Bee I know, and I was just trying to lighten the mood. I don't like the situation any more than you do, it probably scares me the most out of anyone. I don't want to lose you, I just don't want to dwell on the possibility either." He looked into her eyes pleading, "Can you please try and understand that?"

Bethany just squeezed his hand, she couldn't bring herself to say anything for fear of losing all emotional control. That night they played gin for an hour or two before Perez returned. Bailey ran and greeted her friend at the door when he entered. Bethany stood up from the floor while Kevin cleaned up the cards.

"Well?" Her voice demanded answers from the man.

Perez helped himself to a drink from the fridge before answering her. "The captain isn't happy, that's for sure. You're pretty much going to be stuck here until the case is solved, it sounded like he's taking you off the case too." Perez saw the anger in Andrew's eyes, "Look, I'm really sorry but that was a very personal threat, the captain doesn't want to take any risks."

"He's going to have to lock me up then, tomorrow morning I'm going into the station and there's nothing he can say or do to stop me. You either Perez!" Bethany challenged Kevin, "Don't you even try to stop me, and I swear I will ship you back to Boyertown in a heartbeat! Do not mess with me, either of you!" Bethany raised her hand and was about to say something else but shook her head and instead went into her bedroom.

She could feel the anger building inside of her. One of these days she was going to snap and then they'd really be worried. She was just tired of everyone micro-managing her life! First her uncle and now the captain. Kevin was probably one of the worst offenders. Andrews was really starting to feel letting him back in her life was a mistake.

The guys left her alone for the night and set themselves on the couch. They watched TV, distracting them from the day's events. At one point, Kevin decided he was going to try doing some research again and helped himself to Bee's laptop. He went straight to google and started searching for experts on earthworms. It was his own theory that the person responsible for those murders knew about the annelids on a scientific level. Kevin knew the possibility of finding anything didn't even exist, but it made him feel better knowing he was at least trying. It pained him to watch Bethany look beaten every day and everyone feeling hopeless. Tiring himself, he only searched for an hour or so before heading to bed himself. Kevin checked in on a sleeping Bee, kissing her on the forehead and then laying down on the floor beside the bed and drifting asleep.

Chapter 8: Blood Worm

Bee woke up the next morning surprisingly feeling quite refreshed. She looked below her and saw Kevin laying there still sleeping soundly. She pulled onto her robe and went into the kitchen area as quietly as possible she opened up the fridge to start pulling out the eggs and milk and preparing French toast. After grabbing the skillet, she walked over into the living room and saw what they had been working on the night before. The laptop was still on and she saw paperwork covered by the side of it with notes jotted down about people who were earthworm specialists. She thought it was clever of him to come up with a new angle to the case, but she didn't think it was relevant to the murders. Suppose, though the earthworms are more of a signature and least likely to be an occupation. Something else to look into later.

Heading back to the kitchen to get the bread into the mixture of eggs and milk and put in the skillet, frying it. Annoyed Perez looked up from his position on the couch, he sat up quickly and sniffed the air. He smiled, "Bee, something smells good, would you be cooking us some breakfast? No one would have known you were a regular Susie Homemaker."

"That would be French toast" she said, flipping over another piece on the skillet. "How did you sleep last night?" she asked Perez.

"Not bad. Your couch is surprisingly comfy." Perez noted.

Kevin emerged from the bedroom, yawning and rubbing his eyes. He smiled when he caught Bee's glance. Then, just like Perez had done, Kevin sniffed the air and smiled even broader. "Mmm, Bee's famous French toast. You know Perez, she got this recipe from her grandmother and it's the best French toast I've ever had the pleasure of eating."

"Oh yeah?" Perez turned from Kevin to Andrews, "What's the secret ingredient? All grandmothers add something a little special to all their recipes."

"The secret is adding a bit of love Perez!" She laughed at the scrunched face Perez made.

Bee sat two plates down on the table for the boys to eat. She went back into the kitchen and began to make herself some breakfast. "Now you boys need to hurry up and eat so we can all get down to the station."

Kevin and Perez looked at each other before both shaking their heads and looking back at Andrews. "No can do detective," Perez spoke up. "I'm on strict orders to have you on lock down and not let you leave this apartment. It's for your own safety."

"I'm with him Bee, it isn't safe for you to be out on the streets right now. At least, not until they have a little more information about whoever is sending you those letters and flowers. It's best if you just stay here. Bailey and I will keep you company." Kevin pleaded with her.

"I don't need to become a prisoner in my own home Kevin." Bee puts her own French toast on a plate and joined the men at the table. "I want you both to know, that the moment I finish my breakfast I will be out that door and on my way to the station. Are we clear?" Bee pointed her fork at each of them and waited for a nod before continuing to eat.

Perez and Kevin shared a glance. They were in silent agreement that no matter what it would take, they would not let Andrews leave the apartment. Kevin especially was going to make it his task to keep her safe. He wasn't sure what exactly the threat was but he knew that it was enough to keep a guard at the house.

During a moment where everyone was taking a bite, the phone rang. All three checked their respected phones, seeing which one was the one ringing. "Mine." Andrews called out.

Andrews stood and walked away from the table before hitting accept on her phone. "This is Andrews. Yes, sir, Perez is still here. Yes, I was planning on coming into the station shortly. Sir, I'm okay to come in. Sir, please!" She paused to listen. "Yes, sir, I will let Perez know." With that, she hung up the phone.

Perez had been watching the conversation take place. "Andrews what did the captain say?"

"He wants you to bring me into the station. He thinks it'd be safer if they have me in lock up so they can keep an eye on me." Andrews wasn't sure if Perez would believe her or not but she had to try anyways.

"Alright, sounds good. When you're done with your breakfast then we'll head out. Kevin, if you feel the need, you can tag along. I'm sure you can hole up at Andrews' desk till the captain releases her." Perez finished his last bite of the French toast and then carried his plate to the sink. "I'm ready when you are."

A little later, the three were on their way into the station. Perez took Andrews in his squad car, and had Kevin following him close behind. Walking into the station, a few of the officers stopped and watched the three walk back toward the captain's office. Andrews controlled her urge to say something to the gawkers, it was becoming like spectacle and she couldn't stand it.

Captain Harris was not surprised when Andrews walked into his office. "Perez, how could you let her come here against my orders?"

"Sir, she said you told her to come into the station." Perez showed slight fear and surprise.

The captain shook his head, "Of course, she would never lie to you when it involves not being able to come into the station and defying orders." Harris looked at Andrews, "She would never be dishonest about what her superior told her to do."

"Next time can you just call me?" Perez asked the captain.

The captain smiled, knowing he should have done just that. Perez apologized to the captain before leaving the room, glaring at Andrews on the way out. The captain motioned for Andrews and Kevin to take a seat. He then picked up the phone and dialed for Baker to come join them. They didn't have to wait long before Baker joined them. Captain Harris picked up a file and gave it to Andrews.

"Ok, so to review, both of the girls were killed on March 7th in the morning. The next victim wasn't killed, then until Saturday the 11th. That's quite a few days in between." Andrews noted from the file. "If this was a serial killer, they normally escalate as time goes on. Could it be there's another victim, and we just haven't found them yet?"

Baker took the file from Andrews, "Have any calls come in from someone else missing from the retirement home? Maybe it goes in two's? Both girls came from the same apartment complex on the UB campus, perhaps there's another resident missing and they just haven't been reported yet."

Captain Harris leaned back in his chair, "We can't assume anything yet, we need to try and get ahead of this though."

"The autopsy report hasn't been released yet for the latest victim, but we know both girls had a last meal of earthworms before they died which caused them to regurgitate." Baker announced. "Norm said he found some sort of burns on their throats to support that."

Andrews picked up where Baker left off, "And then Frank said the worms from Leah were not from the same area that Frankie's worms were. Then again, they were found at different locations? Could that be why?" She scrunched her face, "I really am not a worm expert."

Rubbing his brow the captain gave his next command, "I want you two to look into this a little further. I don't want us looking into the worms if it's got nothing to do with the case. I appreciated your nursery rhyme theory earlier Andrews but if this is a dead end, let's not waste any more time on it. You're both dismissed."

Before anyone could stand, Junior came in and handed a note to Harris. "Sir a tip just came in to this address. The person on the phone said we should go check it out that it's connected to the serial killer Worm."

Andrews noticed Junior seemed to be sweating a lot and appeared uncomfortable. "Junior you doing okay?" She asked him.

He seemed surprised that she asked and went into a description of his symptoms. The captain looked at the rookie and tried to get him to realize that no one cared. Junior wasn't paying attention and when through his whole more through a very elaborate story. Once he finished, he excused himself and left the room with the others still in shock.

Ignoring Junior she stood and moved behind the captain so she could read the address. "6545 Belle Way, Clarence. That's not too far from here. Baker and I can go check it out."

"Why don't you take a few officers with you in case it turns into something, let me know if you find anything." The captain handed the address to Andrews before dismissing everyone from his office.

"Kevin why don't you go back to the apartment and check on Bailey." Andrews told him.

"I can do that." Kevin replied, "Let me know when you guys get back and I'll come over."

Andrews nodded, "Will do."

On the way over to the location, Andrews pulled up the address on her phone. "The house belongs to a woman named Marion Cullen. She's 68, retired and looks like she lives alone."

"Well, let's go check on Ms. Cullen and make sure she's doing okay." Baker drove to the location of the note and pulled into the driveway.

The house sat back from the road, it was a small ranch house that seemed to be lacking in upkeep. The yard was overgrown with weeds. The house could have used a new coat of paint and the screen door seemed to be falling off the hinges. It appeared as though no one had lived here in a while. Two officers exited their squad car and followed Baker and Andrews to the front door.

Whispering, Baker gave instructions to the other officers, "You two go around back and check for movement or signs of life. Andrews and I are going to enter from the front. Radio in if you run into trouble."

Andrews tried the front door and found it was unlocked. She stood back and let Baker enter first, gun out. The entry way splits off into the kitchen or the living room. The detectives saw the other officers coming in through a door that lead into the living room so Andrews motioned toward the kitchen. She entered the room first and scanned, there was no one there.

Plates were stacked in the sink and it appeared as though someone had finished a meal and just left it on the table. Mice were covering the scraps. The detectives continued moving through the kitchen into the dining room. It was a museum of silver, china, covered in dust. Nothing else seemed out of place. The house seemed to break apart into different rooms from there.

"Spread out, everyone takes a room. Call if you find anything." Baker barked at the others there.

Andrews went into what looked like the study. She ran her fingers over the bookcase, seeing that it had a layer of dust on it. The books were old classics, nothing out of the ordinary. In the far corner was a desk. She figured this would be a good place to start searching. On top of the desk were blank sheets of paper. Unlike everything else so far in the house, the desk was clean. There wasn't any dust and it looked like someone had been here recently.

The stationary on top the desk appeared familiar. It took Andrews only a moment to realize where she had seen it. It was the same paper that her notes had been written on. Sure, there could be paper like this all over, but the watermark on it was distinct and she had a gut feeling this was it.

"Baker! Get over here now!" Andrews screamed for her partner.

Baker came rushing into the room, gun out until he saw Andrews and then he lowered his weapon. "What did you find?"

Andrews now starting to feel numb held up the paper, "It's the stationary Geoff. It's the stationary that damn psychopath has been writing those letters on."

He took the paper from Andrews and looked at it carefully, "We should send this back to the lab to be checked but I think you're right. Have you found anything else?"

"No." She quietly answered. "Nothing."

Baker helped Andrews search the rest of the study. In one of the drawers there were more letters. Andrews' hand shook as she pulled them out and handed them to Baker. There must have been about five of them, written out and ready to go. They had sticky notes on them with numbers, but they weren't chronological. They didn't make sense to either Baker or Andrews.

"He lives here Baker! We were in his house!" Andrews began getting emotional, "Call it in Baker, I want this house searched top to bottom and that creep found! Now Baker!"

He pulled her into his arms, "I will Bethany, I'll call for back up but you need to calm down. If it gets back to the captain that you're having a breakdown over this case, you'll be pulled and I know that's the last thing you want right now. Take a deep breath."

One of the other officers came into the room and announced, "Detectives we have a deceased woman in the bedroom, looks like she's been dead a while."

Baker let her go and shook his head. He dialed on his phone and called the captain. "Sir, we're going to need back up at the Belle Way location. It looks like this house is connected to the case after all. Also, you'll need to contact Norm, we have a body on scene."

Once he hung up the phone, both Baker and Andrews followed the other officer through the house to the bedroom. There, just like he had told them, there was a lady dead on the bed. She was already partly decomposed with rats and mice all over her body. There were maggots showing through her orifices, and skin falling off the bones. It was obvious she had been there for quite a while. The bed and sheets were stained with blood. The scene itself was grotesque in nature and smelled of rotting flesh.

The rest of the room was covered in feces and dust. The window had been painted black with no curtains. There was a chair in the corner with a book on it that hadn't been touched for a while. They checked the closet which had women's clothes hanging in it, dating back a few decades. The dresser didn't have much of anything on it, just a few pieces of jewelry.

Andrews couldn't handle standing there anymore and left the room. She needed some fresh air so she went out the back door into the garden. Unlike the front of the house, it was pruned and taken care of. There were fresh flowers growing and it smelled amazing. She went deeper into the garden under a lattice worked archway, covered in ivy.

There was a shed back behind the flowers. With her hand on her gun, she opened the door of the shed slowly and entered. Covering the walls were shelves full of roses. Behind the door was a spool of red ribbon and a vat of black dye. Andrews collapsed at the sight, unable to breathe. Geoff ran through the garden when he heard her scream. He watched as she felt unable to get to her fast enough. Andrews heard him call for her, but he sounded so far away, she felt herself losing consciousness until at last she fainted and her world went dark.

"Bethany! Bethany wakes up!" Baker shook his partner and checked for a pulse.

Coming to, Andrews opened her eyes to see the look of fear on Baker's face. "What happened to you?" He asked her as he helped her sit up.

"I found the roses." She pointed behind him. "Behind you are the dye and the ribbon."

"I see it." Baker stood, pulling her up with him. "You need to stand, we'll have one of the other officers take you home so you can rest."

"No!" She snapped at him. "I'm not going anywhere. You saw that lady in bed, that's probably the guy's mother and look at what he did to her. I don't even what to think about what he has planned for me. I want to stay, we need to catch him."

Baker pulled her away from the shed and called for one of the other officers to process the scene. "Let's continue looking around the house."

The two bathrooms and the garage held nothing but dusty evidence that someone had once lived there. Andrews and Baker found the cellar door in the hallway outside the bedroom. Guns drawn they opened the door and flipped on the lights. There were footprints in the dust leading down the steps. They went down into the basement and found there were more rooms than most people have in a rancher. What appeared to be a library was the first room. It wasn't dusty like the study had been, and the shelves were stocked with books. Half the shelves seemed to be about entomology and insects alone, while the rest was media related and books based on true crimes. It was a serial killer's research center.

Baker went over to one of the cabinets in the library and opened the doors. "Andrews gets over here, there's something you should see."

She cautiously moved over to where the cabinet stood and looked at what her partner had found. Rows and rows of jars covered the shelves. They weren't empty either. Each jar had about four inches of dirt in the jar. Andrews pulled one off the shelf with the label #5 on it. She spun it around and peered into the glass jar, only to see something wriggling inside. She should have known better, of course, there'd be worms inside. Of course the person who was sending her letters and flowers would be either in connection to the serial killer they were looking for, or the actual serial killer.

Taking the jar from her hand, Baker turned Andrews to face him. "You're done. I'm taking you off the case, you're going straight home and you're not leaving your apartment until I tell you that you're allowed to."

"Don't even try it Geoff, I'm okay. This is getting weird, really weird, but I'm okay." She wasn't sure if she meant it or not, but she knew she had to stay on the case.

"There's still more rooms to search, let's keep moving. If there's something else though that sets you off, you're going home and I don't care what you say." Baker gave her a stern look. "Am I clear Andrews?"

"Yes." She agreed.

The two continued to the other side of the library, through the door and into the next room. They had entered another bedroom, nothing special about this one. Simple cot in the corner and a nightstand with a lamp. Someone had definitely been there recently, the bed wasn't made. The detectives searched under the bed and in the night stand, finding nothing. Continuing into the next room, Baker reached to turn on the light. A red glow filled the room.

"It's a dark room," Andrews realized.

Around the room was a string with pictures dangling from it. On the back wall were pictures posted and labels. Baker and Andrews were overwhelmed by the sight. On the back wall were pictures of their now four victims. Leah, Frankie, Charlie and Marion all had an "x" over their faces. It was as though they had been stalked leading up to their death. There were pictures of them out shopping and eating with friends. There was a picture of the girls walking to class and Charlie participating in a chess game in the retirement home. Their entire lives in the past month had been documented and posted onto the wall. The pictures were all labeled with a date and location.

Andrews noticed them at the edge of the wall were a set of new pictures. There was a young woman, late twenties maybe, she was in a yoga outfit leaving the YMCA. Under a few pictures of her was her name, Dana Whitman. Unlike the other pictures though, there weren't any "x's" over hers.

"Baker, I think this is the next victim. We need to find her." Andrews got out a pad of paper and started writing down the girl's name and a description.

After clearing his throat, "Actually Andrews, I believe we have our next few victims."

Andrews turned around and noticed Baker pointing to the pictures that had been hanging up, the ones that weren't labeled yet. She walked over to him and looked up at the pictures. There were many young women and random adults in the pictures. A little farther down the line she finally saw what had gotten Baker's attention, it was a picture of her. It wasn't a new picture either, it must have been from over a year ago back when she was home.

"I don't recognize that building in the background, where did they get this picture of you?" Baker questioned.

Andrews was beginning to get frustrated with all this nonsense, "That's New Hanover Park, I used to play softball at that field with the police department. This is a picture from 2009, before Corey ever became an issue."

"Well, I think it's pretty clear that we aren't dealing with Corey and his crew anymore. This goes beyond them." Baker wasn't sure who yet but he knew no drug dealing thugs could be behind all this.

"I see the two of you have been keeping ourselves busy." A man started walking into the dark room.

Baker spun around, "Captain Harris, I wasn't expecting you to come down here."

"I wasn't going to but then I heard there was another body and that the stationary and roses were found here. I wanted to check in and make sure everyone was hanging in there." Captain Harris looked over at Andrews. "And how exactly are the two of you holding up?"

"Well, take a look over here captain. Looks like there's another victim, probably within the next few days. Then we found all of these, there's at least thirty different pictures hanging up here, one of them is me." Andrews got the captain caught up.

Harris walked over to the wall and took down one of the pictures of Dana with the label. "Get this back to the station ASAP and try to locate this lady before she ends up on the slab with the others. I'll get the guys over here to finish processing the entire house. I want to know everything about this lady and the house."

"Will do Sir" Baker replied.

"Get a few squad cars out here too, and watch to see who takes this road, he's got to come back eventually, and his menacing plan is here." Captain Harris left the room and sent two officers in to finish processing the scene.

Baker and Andrews made their way back to their car, passing by what seemed like the entire department sweeping the house. Andrews noticed Junior and a few of the other rookie officers standing outside the bedroom making jokes about Ms. Cullen's body. She started walking in their direction to say something, but was pulled back by her partner. He shook his head at her and they continued to the cars. It was a silent ride back to the station, as they both went over in their head what all they had seen at the house.

"What now? We have one name, what about all those other pictures he was hanging up?" Andrews was shaking with frustration. "I just don't see either what they all have in common. They were completely random people. None of them looked alike or looked like they would even know each other."

"I know Andrews, but we'll figure it out. We always do." Baker hoped he sounded more confident than he was actually feeling.

Sighing, "You don't know. How could you possibly know that this is all going to be okay? Serial Killers are supposed to have a type, he doesn't have a type. How can we figure out his pattern if he doesn't have a stupid type?"

"Calm down Bethany. We will figure it out. Trust me." Baker did his best to get a smile out.

The rest of the ride they were silent. Arriving at the station, Andrews could already see Kevin had been there the entire time. They both walked into the station and headed back to their desks. Andrews sat down and put her head in her hands. Wasn't long before she had someone behind her, holding her tight and whispering in her ear. She knew it was him, but right now she needed to focus and not have whatever he was to her now there as a distraction.

"Kevin, please you need to go find something to do. Geoff and I have a lot we need to get done this evening if we're going to catch whoever is doing this. We need to beat them to Dana." She lifted her head and spun her chair so she could look at him. "Please Kevin, you need to let us work. Please."

"Ok Bee, all you had to do was ask. I'll wait over in the waiting room if you need anything." He kissed her on the forehead and walked out toward the waiting area. He could tell she was hurting, but knew better than to push it.

Baker took the board where they had the timeline and all the information into the conference room down the hall. "Come on, we're going to need to spread out."

The two detectives worked well into the night trying to search for Dana Whitman, with no prevail. They had tried every search database known to try and find this woman. The board was now littered with notes and diagrams trying to piece together what had been found at Ms. Cullen's house. Too many questions and not enough answers drove Andrews to finally just throw up her hands in desperation.

"I give up! I just give up. What are we doing wrong?" She was extremely frustrated with the turn of events.

"We aren't doing anything wrong. Sometimes this is just how these things go. Think of the Zodiac Killer, they still aren't sure who that is." This wasn't Baker's first time but he was feeling useless as well.

Andrews stood, "Maybe we should go check in with Norm and see if he has any news from the last two victims."

"It's 11 at night, I bet we're the only ones left." Baker snickered. "Not everyone is as dedicated or obsessed as we are with this case."

"I didn't realize it was so late," Andrews finally looked at the clock. "You should get home to Val."

Baker shook his head, "Don't you worry about me and Val, she told me to stay with you and she doesn't want to see me again till the guy is caught. You know she loves you like her own daughter, she wants me to make sure you're safe."

"Well, I appreciate it." Just then Andrews remembered, "Wait, I bet there's at least one other person still here."

"I'll go get him for you."

"Thanks Baker, maybe a fresh perspective will help?" Andrews was exhausted at this point and could barely think straight.

Baker eventually came back with Kevin. "You were right Andrews, he was still there."

"I thought you had forgotten about me." Kevin teased her.

Andrews made a face in response, "We're thinking you may be able to help us."

"Not sure why you think that, but go ahead." He was puzzled as to why they were asking him, but would do anything to try and help find the guy who's after Bee.

Baker pointed to the board, "So far there are four victims. The first two are from the UB campus, the third of the retirement home and then the last one we just found earlier today in her home."

"As far as we know they don't have any connection, there's no trends." Andrews picked up.

Kevin looked over the board, trying himself to piece everything together. "Do the worms have anything to do with it or was it all just a coincidence with the first two murders?"

Baker and Andrews exchanged looks, "We actually aren't sure yet, and we don't have the autopsy report back yet from the last two victims. We don't know if there were worms found there as well." Baker informed him.

"Okay, but you have noted up here that you found jars of worms in this house you just visited?" Kevin pointed to the board. "Don't you think it's a bit odd that you found jars of worms in this house and there were worms with the first two murders?"

"Sue Baker! I told them the worms would have something to do with it, and they all laughed at me saying it was a waste of my time to look into it." Andrews was rather pleased with herself for picking up on that earlier.

Baker shook his head, "Doesn't mean their significant."

"Well, it could!" Andrews paused to think, "They could be his call sign. Kevin thought that up the other morning and now I'm thinking it's a possibility."

Baker again shook his head, "What else do you notice Kevin?"

"It seems that none of the suspects have anything in common either. The only thing people have in common with this whole case is," Kevin paused, "that it all revolves around that house."

Andrews didn't hear that last bit from Kevin, she was off in her own thought. "What if it's more a hit for hire. There's the one murderer who lives at the house and people who wanted all those victims dead, went to him to do the deed."

"Well, that's possible Andrews but do you think it'd be this complex of a system?" Baker asked.

"How am I supposed to know? This is the first type of serial killer, the crazy man case I've worked on." Andrews shot back.

Baker looked at the clock and then proposed, "How about I go make us some coffee and we look at what was found at the house again and see if we can find another connection."

"Deal." His partner responded. "We should look into who Ms. Cullens knew, too, track down her son."

"Captain already has people looking into that," Baker replied, "We're supposed to focus on the next victim and the connection."

"Oh, okay," Andrews finished letting Baker go make coffee.

It was nearing one in the morning, it had been a long day for all of them, but they were getting hopefully a little bit closer. The board was beginning to get cluttered with sticky notes of different questions that didn't seem to have answers. There seemed to be no way to move forward in the case. Andrews was looking forward to morning so she could ask Norm what he had found out. The rest of the force was probably still processing the house, she knew the captain would let up until they knew everything possible. Dana was still out there and as far as anyone knew, she was alive. They had to do all in their means to try and find her, before it was too late.

Chapter 9: Tiger Worm

A few moments later, Baker returned with coffee for all of them. It was now nearing two am and they still haven't heard from the captain or anyone else. It was as though thinking about it, willed the phone to ring. Andrews answered and motioned for Baker to come near her. She then put the phone on speaker so they could all hear.

"Captain, I got you on speaker. Baker and I are here." She motioned for Kevin to stay quiet. She didn't think the captain would have a problem with Kevin being involved but now was not the time to bring it up.

"We're still processing the scene, but I had a feeling you two wouldn't be at home but still at the station working. Have you come up with anything else?" He sounded exhausted over the phone.

Baker pushed the phone toward Andrews, "Tell him your current theory."

"Ok," she stated hesitantly, "I'm thinking maybe the person living at Belle Way was a hit man and maybe that's why the victims don't have anything in common."

"Hit men normally don't kill in a row though or act like a serial killer. Do you have an explanation for that yet?" Captain Harris questioned.

"No sir, we haven't really gotten too far on the current evidence. We've just been trying to come up with explanations of why things are taking place the way they are.

Captain Harris sighed into the phone, "Alright. Here we've uncovered a lot more than what was originally expected. It seems like this house is the center of everything taking place. There are addresses and photos all over the basement of the house. I've sent a few officers back to the station to get working on the new leads. Junior should be bringing you two some leads for you to follow up on. Please call me if anything turns up, I'm going to stay here until the search of the house is complete."

Andrews picked up the phone and took it off speaker, "Yes sir, we'll let you know if the leads come up with anything. Let us know if you need any assistance back at the house."

There was a click on the other end of the phone, the captain had hung up. Andrews put her phone down and ran her fingers through her hair. "Guess this means we have more work to do in a little bit."

As soon as she said that, Baker's phone started ringing. Baker looked at the number on his phone, "its Norm."

"Well, what are you waiting for pick up?" Andrews told him.

"Baker here," he answered. After listening for a while he replied back, "Ok, we'll be there in a bit."

Andrews tilted her head when she saw the expression on Baker's face, "What's wrong?"

"There's been another murder, it could be Dana." He lowered his head.

"Crap." Andrews grabbed her things, "Well let's go."

Kevin caught the look Bee gave him, "Don't worry, I'll stay put and read a book or something."

"If Junior gets back with the evidence, let him know we're at another murder location." Andrews instructed Kevin.

"Got it."

"And don't touch anything!" She warned.

Kevin gave her a look. "I'm not a child."

"Fine." Andrews finished as she and Baker left.

Andrews and Baker got in their car and rode to the address Norm had given them. Andrews checked the GPS on the location, "1095 Youngs Rd looks to be a townhouse apartment in Amherst."

"Norm said it was apartment B so that makes sense." Baker looked over at his partner. "He also said it was a middle aged woman."

Andrews' heart sank, "Do you think it's Dana?"

"I can't be sure but it's sounding like a possibility."

They arrive at the scene and see that tape has already been strung up. There were reporters lined up by the tape, probably causing mass hysteria at this point. Baker saw Norm in the distance and watched as he waved them over. They both noticed that everyone seemed to be wearing those goofy booties which meant there was probably a mess of blood inside the apartment. Walking through the door, the observation was supported. Norm handed both detectives a set of booties before showing them into the living room.

"Welcome to hell, detectives." Norm crouched by the victim and opened her hand with his pen. "I'd like to introduce you two, to our fifth victim of Worm's, Ms. Dana Whitman. I believe you've all heard that name before."

Andrews had to turn from the scene and get a grip on her emotions, "Shit."

"It's a damn shame is what it is." Norm stood up and faced the detectives. "Call came in about a half hour ago, a friend was staying over with her and heard some noise. They came out of the bedroom to find Dana like this. No one else was here."

"Who exactly was the one that found her?" Baker looked around but didn't see anyone being questioned.

Norm pointed to a woman sitting in the kitchen. "That's Nancy Holden, she said she's another Zumba instructor."

"Let's go talk to her then," Baker said to Andrews. "First though, Norm did you find anything out of the ordinary with this one?"

"This was a hit to the head. There's a broken vase scattered around the body. Someone hit our victim from behind and that's how the blood got sprayed about the room. She's missing part of her skull so there must have been something else used, we have yet to find anything that could cause this kind of damage." Norm paused to move the victim's head a little. "She has strangulation marks on her neck as well, like the other girls had. Other than that, the worm is the only thing that connects her to the other cases. I'll know more after an autopsy."

"Sounds like the killer went a little overboard this time." Baker noted.

Andrews agreed, "Well he's definitely escalating that's for sure."

Baker and Andrews excused themselves and went over to talk to Nancy. Andrews noticed the woman seemed aged by the situation, she had bags under her eyes and they were red and puffy, as though she had been crying for hours. Pure exhaustion showed on the woman's defeated face. Andrews couldn't help but feel bad for her. Having to wake up to such a horrific sight would give anyone nightmares and cause them to have demons of their own, memories that they could never forget.

"Ma'am, we're detectives with the Buffalo Police department, do you mind if we ask you a few questions?" Baker asked the woman.

Nancy looked up at the detective, "I've already been asked more questions than I cared to answer. Go ahead though, ask away, I'm not allowed to go anywhere. Maybe it'll help pass the time."

Andrews looked at the woman, "I get it, you're tired and you've see something we all wished wasn't real. Do you remember anything from right before the time you found Dana in the living room?"

"No." Nancy's eyes started to glisten as tears formed, "I just remember hearing a crash and I came into the living room and found Dana on the floor. There was blood everywhere." She started breathing irregular and crying uncontrollably.

"Ma'am, we're going to need you to stay calm." Baker attempted to get the woman's attention back.

Andrews sat in the chair in front of Nancy, "How did you know her?"

"We met at Zumba, she was my instructor and helped me become one myself a week ago. I was staying here because my husband-"Nancy trailed off and became more hysterical.

"What about your husband Nancy?" Baker questioned her, "what does he have to do with this? Did he hurt Dana?"

"No, no he wouldn't. He didn't know, he had no idea where I was hiding." Nancy sobbed.

Andrews and Baker shared a glance, "I think we have enough for now. Let's find out who talked to her first, maybe they got more out of her."

Baker nodded in agreement, "Alright."

The two detectives walked outside to where a group of uniforms were standing around. "Which one of you talked with Ms. Holden inside?" Baker asked the group.

"That would be me sir." A young new recruit stated.

Andrews spoke up, "What did she tell you about her husband?"

The rookie turned toward Andrews, "Not much Ma'am, she was a little hysterical when we talked to her. What I could make out though is that he beat her and she ran away and was staying with Dana."

"Didn't she happen to mention anyone that would want to hurt Dana?" Baker asked.

"No, sir. Not a thing."

"Ok well thank you for your help." Baker stated before walking away from the group.

Andrews followed Baker back to the squad car. "What are you thinking?"

"Could be a jealous husband out for revenge. Maybe he thought Dana stole Nancy away from him? That would keep with your theory pretty nicely." Baker offered.

"Maybe." Andrews was no longer sure how her theory worked. "Let's head back to the station and see what the captain had given Junior for us. We can add this new information to the board and see if there's anything we missed."

Arriving back at the station Andrews asked the receptionist if Junior was back yet or if there were any messages for her or Baker. She was handed back a note. Andrews recognized the stationary immediately. Apparently no one had told the staff here about what was found in the house and not to accept anything from any messengers. Andrews questioned whether it would be worth asking any questions.

Before she could say anything Baker spoke up, "Why don't we head back to the conference room?" It was more of a statement than a question.

On the way back to the conference room, Andrews stopped Baker. "Why didn't you ask her about the letter?"

"At this point, I'm not inclined to trust anyone. You shouldn't be either."

"Alright." For now the answer satisfied her.

They got back to the conference room and found Kevin surrounded by papers, he was furiously writing. When he saw the detectives entering the conference room, he quickly got up and ran over to Andrews. He hugged her tight and then escorted her back to the table.

"You've been busy haven't you?" Andrews flipped through the pages on the table. "Care to explain what you're been up to?"

"Well I was just mapping out the letter part to all this. Bee you got a letter when you first got here and then again after the two girls were killed." Kevin waited.

"Ok I follow you." Andrews' interest had been sparked.

Kevin continued, "You got the most recent then after Charlie's death. It all goes together somehow. I saw in your notes too that you found more letters in that woman's house, along with stationary. I think you'll get a new letter each time there's a victim."

"Actually, there's been another one." Andrews handed the note to Baker to add to the board. "It said: Got a little held up the past few days but don't worry, I haven't forgotten about you."

"So there is a pattern. Those letters are connected to the murders." Kevin sat down, "Bee, I'm sorry. I was really hoping I was wrong and it was just a shot in the dark."

"Looks like you're spot on Kevin. Congrats." Andrews too sat down.

Baker leaned on the table, "I want both of you to snap out of it. This thing is far from over and we all need to keep our heads in the game."

Just then four officers walked by the door of the conference room, escorting a woman. She was screaming out to be released. Baker quickly moved to the door and looked out. He couldn't see who they were taking into the interrogation room. The captain was close behind and saw Baker peering out of the conference room.

He came over and opened the door as Baker stepped aside. "You two might want to follow me." Harris then noticed Kevin sitting at the table, "Mr. Williams if you plan on hanging out and hearing all this confidential information, I'm going to need you to head out to the lobby and ask the receptionist for the consultant paperwork. We'll need you to sign that so we can hold you liable if any of this gets out."

"Understood sir, thank you." Kevin was relieved, he thought he was going to get excused.

The two detectives followed the captain into the interrogation viewing room. That's when they both realized it was Nancy Holden they had in interrogation. Andrews became confused but watched as Nancy screamed and rambled on. She seemed to have lost her mind, more so than Andrews remembered from the house.

"Sir, what is she doing here? She was questioned at the scene." Andrews was really confused as to what was taking place.

The captain turned from the window, "It seems our crazy lady confessed to murdering Dana soon after you both left. She was ranting on about how she did it, and when asked where the murder weapon was she took officers to where she had stashed it."

"I don't understand, what would be her motive for killing Dana?" Baker was now just as confused.

"That's what I want you to find out." The captain turned back toward the window, "We need to get more information out of her but she's too hysterical right now, she won't be able to tell us anything."

It took about twenty minutes for Nancy to finally stop screaming. Andrews and Baker just sat in the viewing room watching as she went from rambling on about nothing, to bawling her eyes out about everything. The scene was interesting to watch someone have a complete breakdown and just lost all sense of what not only was appropriate but what seemed to be reality. Once Nancy had nothing left to get out and the emotions were more under control the detectives decided it was time they go have a talk with her and see what they can find out.

Entering the room, Andrews took point, "Nancy, do you remember us from earlier?"

Nancy shook her head, "Yes."

"Do you know why you're here Ms. Holden?" Andrews asked next.

Nancy looked up from the desk, anger in her eyes, "Because that bitch slept with my husband and thought she could be friends with me to cover it up."

Andrews turned to look at Baker, who had a surprised look on his face, just like she was feeling at that moment. "How do you know she had an affair with your husband?"

"After she thought I fell asleep, I heard her sneak off to the living room. I followed her and heard that bitch talking to my husband on the phone." Nancy gritted the words through her teeth. "He had told me to strangle her, but I didn't think that would be enough, so I bashed her head it. It felt good."

Andrews leaned back to put more distance between her and the crazy lady, "He who? Who told you to strangle her?"

"The man I had talked to. He told me all I needed to do was strangle her and then put the worm in her hand. I had already made her eat that shit he gave me in a jar, mixed it in with the soup and told her I was too upset to eat it myself." Nancy freely gave the information.

Baker walked up to the desk from the corner he had been standing in, "Why are you sharing all this?"

"It's over. My life is over, so why keep it in any longer." Nancy put her head in her hands and didn't utter another word.

Baker and Andrews left the room and stood outside up against the wall for a while. Everything they had thought couldn't be true now. It couldn't possibly be a hit man because this lady just admitted to the murder and knew too much to have been making it up. There were things she had said though that hung on their minds. Someone was pulling the strings, these people were puppets. He was using puppets to kill and leave behind his signature. There has been no serial killer, just some master mind creating murderers and telling them how to do it. The other question was what could possibly have been in the jars that he told her to make them eat? Instead of getting answers, they just got more questions.

Baker motioned to an officer to come take Nancy to a holding cell. They'd wait a few hours before trying to talk to her again. She was still a bundle of nerves. There wasn't much they'd probably get from her at this point. The two walked back to the conference room to wait.

Two hours went by, technically it was finally a decent enough hour that the station was packed with officers and civilians working on the case. The captain had pulled all strings to make sure everyone was working on the Worm case and nothing else. They finally had gotten a break and learned a piece of information that could help them, but nothing actual factual to go off of. There wasn't much they could do without getting more information out of Nancy.

"You ready to go Andrews?" Baker asked ready to go back to talk to Nancy.

Andrews stood from the conference table, "Yeah, let's go get this over with. I doubt that crazy lady will have much more to say, she seems pretty ticked at her husband right now."

The two walked down to the holding cell. After checking in with the guard standing out front they walked down the hall past empty cells. Nancy had started screaming again a little earlier so they moved her to the back so she wouldn't disrupt the entire station. Andrews noticed something was wrong when they were a few feet away, the door was open. The two detectives picked up their pace.

Andrews gasped at the sight, "Geoff she's been shot!"

"Now how they hell does that happen in a police station?" Baker was beyond furious. He screamed for the guard, "Get the hell over here and tell me how you let someone come in here and shoot our suspect!"

Chapter 10: Snakeworm

The guard was more terrified than anything else, he just stuttered. Frustrated, Baker pushed the man out of his way and left the holding cell area. He pushed past many officers as he went down the hallway. Reaching the captain's office, Baker turned to see where Andrews was before turning back to the captain.

"Sir, we have a serious issue. Nancy's been shot while in the holding cell. The guard doesn't remember anything and if he did, he wouldn't be able to talk right now he's just stuttering, useless fool." Baker stopped to catch his breath.

Calmly, the captain leaned forward, "You're telling me, our suspect who was under our protection was murdered in one of our holding cells?"

"Yes, sir, I saw it as well. Someone shot Nancy execution style." Andrews finally caught up to Baker. She had stayed behind to try and calmly talk to the guard. "The guard says the only ones in an out of there all morning had been officers."

"I want those surveillance videos immediately." At that moment, Junior walked past the door, "Junior! I want you to run to tech and grab me the surveillance videos from the holding cell." The captain demanded to know what happened inside his station.

Andrews knew now probably wasn't the best timing but there was going to be a mass of media if this got out. "Sir, we need someone to make a statement before the rumors start and this gets out. They're already talking about copycats and how the police are incompetent, don't let this be another excuse for the media to make us out to be the bad ones."

"You're right, let me call the PR person." The captain said while dialing the phone. He informed those that needed to know what was going on, before giving his attention back to the detectives. "When those tapes get here I want you to put them in immediately and see who did this."

Junior showed up with the tapes, handing them over to Baker before hurriedly leaving. The captain took the DVD from Baker and put it into his computer. He hit the fast forward button until it went to when they put Nancy in the cell. They watched the tape run normally. A few guards come in and out but there wasn't anything out of the ordinary yet. Andrews noticed something suspicious in the video, she moved around behind the captain and pointed out a person on the screen.

"Do you see this? That's Junior acting all weird." Andrews watched as the rookie walked into the holding cell. It looked like Nancy recognized him, and then a bang and she was gone.

"Get me Junior, now!" The captain screamed.

Baker was already ahead of him and left the office on the hunt for Junior. He came back a short time later, alone. "He's gone sir. The receptionist said he handed her a note this morning and then she didn't see him again till he ran out of the station like someone was chasing him."

"Wait, he gave her a letter this morning?" Andrews looked from the captain to Baker, "He's the one giving me letters, he's been the one this entire time!"

The next five minutes seemed to be on fast forward. Officers were running around, people were screaming orders. The station was in a sense of chaos. No one seemed to actually be doing anything productive. It was as if they were all in a state of shock that a murderer and possible the one they've been searching for the entire time had been among them. It came to light that no one truly knew anything about Junior, they all had thought he was obnoxious enough to stay away from him. Even the captain didn't know much about the rookie other than he was a screw up.

Baker and Andrews met back up in the conference room. Someone had brought in another white board, dedicated specifically only to Junior. They had the past few days all laid out with everything he had a hand in highlighted. He not only was the one who had been associated with all the letters but he also was the one that had handed the captain the address for Ms. Cullen's house. What did it mean though?

Andrews stared at the board, before voicing her thoughts. "It's been a game, hasn't it? Junior not only has been handing us the cards as he's wanted us to find them but that house- It was all set up for us to find the house."

"It does seem like things have fallen into our laps as we've needed them to." Baker was beginning to doubt himself. "We should have picked up on it earlier."

"We didn't know what to look for though. We can't start blaming ourselves, we need to get on this and figure out what's going on." Andrews did not think this was the time to start doubting each other.

"Right now there are people out looking for Junior. Why don't we go to his apartment and start there ourselves. He's probably already cleaned it out since he had a head start but it's something." Baker grabbed his coat and they both left the conference room.

Kevin had left when the mayhem had started to stay out of the way. He agreed to be back in a few hours to check on Andrews and bring dinner around for the detectives. They all swore to live at the station until this was solved. They had a lead but then Junior killed their lead so they were left with nothing but to try and figure out what part Junior played in all this.

Arriving at Junior's apartment, the first thing the detectives noticed is that it smelled. A squirrely looking man kept peering out of a door farther down the hallway. The moment the detectives would look over, the door would shut. It would open again then a minute later with the same squirrely man peeking out of the door again.

"Why don't you go figure out what that's all about, it's getting weird." Andrews asked Baker.

Baker walked over to where the door kept opening, "Buffalo Police. Sir, we're trying to conduct an investigation, do you need something?"

"I was actually going to ask you that. I'm Thomas." The man said before closing his door a bit more. "Thomas Newman."

"Well, Thomas Newman, it was nice to meet you. Do you happen to know the man that was staying the apartment two doors down from you?" Baker questioned.

Thomas opened the door a smidge before responding, "Of course I know him. I know them all. I manage them. That was Junior Cullen's apartment."

Andrews looked at Baker, "I thought Junior's last name was, well no actually I don't think I even knew his last name."

"Yeah his name tag just said Junior, which I thought was his last name." Baker answered

Thomas jumped him, "No, definitely was a Cullen's. He was the easiest to manage."

Andrew thought that was an odd way to phrase it, but this guy didn't exactly seem normal in any sense. "Do you happen to have the key to his apartment so we may search it?"

Baker held up a warrant which caused the man to slam the door shut. "I really hope I don't have to arrest this man." He commented while banging on the door. "Sir, please open the door!"

"I was just getting the key." Thomas looked at them like they had done something wrong.

He walked down to Junior's apartment while up against the wall. He checked behind him more times than he seemed to blink, it was constant. Andrews slowed her pace, she was becoming increasingly intrigued by this man. He was a mix of a cockroach and well, no that was it. He reminded her of a cockroach.

As Thomas put the key in the door he added his own sound effects to his turning of the key. He swung the door open, "Hello Junior Mints, it's the Newman show and the Johnny Blues."

Andrews mouthed the word crazy to Baker who had to hold back a laugh. "Buffalo Police, Junior we've all been looking for you. Are you here?"

There was no response coming from the apartment. The detectives entered and began to do a quick search, making sure Junior wasn't there. It was filthy, clothes were thrown about the room, there were dishes piled in the sink and over the counter. Andrews was pretty sure she saw a few mice run across the kitchen floor. The place was a sty, she didn't want to search any farther it made her want to drink Lysol so she could be sure she was clean.

"Baker, seriously, do you think we'll find anything here? Junior clearly isn't home. Can we just call in the crime unit and have them search this place, it's giving me the heeby jeebies." Andrews had gotten out her pen and was lifting papers on a side table, trying hard not to touch anything.

Baker called Andrews over to look at a picture he had found. Surprisingly it was a picture of Junior with the woman they had found at worm's house. He must be related to Ms. Cullen's then or at least knew her well enough to keep a picture of them.

The detectives eventually gave up the search and called for the crime scene unit to come in and finish up. They headed back to the station to piece everything together from that day. It had been a lot to take in all at once. What they needed to do now was step back, take some time off and then come back at it fresh and start over. When they got back to the station, it seemed the captain was already thinking what they were. They both curled up in an empty office and crashed. It had been days since either got a good night sleep and the fatigue was something they could no longer fight.

Andrews awoke first and saw Baker was still sleeping. She snuck out of the office and into the conference room. Andrews pulled everything off the board and piled it all by victim. The way they were going about this was all wrong, it wasn't working. Andrews decided the only way to start over was to literally take everything down and start over. They knew now that the murders were both connected and separate.

She sorted through what was now strewn across the table and put back on the board, all the information they had on Leah. One murder at a time seemed the way to go. Leah died on the 7th around 8am. Her dad was a congressman and her mom was an author and a professor. Neither of them had motive, nor a reason they would want their daughter dead?

At this point the main suspect for Leah's murder was her professor that she had been seeing, Karl Montgomery. Being her advisor, he must have seen her more than normal. Maybe it was a jealousy issue? Andrews wasn't exactly sure what the motive was but she was determined to find out. Last time they had interviewed Dr. Montgomery he left and pulled the lawyer card. It was probably time to bring him back in for another interview.

Baker found his way to the conference room, rubbing his eyes. "Figure anything out while I was dead to the world?"

"Well," she paused, "I think we need to start over." Andrews pointed to the board. "I reworked what we had on Leah. I think we need to call her professor back in. I don't think Junior was capable of killing all those people. At least he couldn't have done it alone."

Sitting down at the table, Baker looked over what Andrews had been working on. "I see. We really don't have anything on him do we?"

Took about two hours but before long Andrews and Baker were staring down Dr. Montgomery through the glass. He was sitting in the interrogation room with his lawyer, tapping his fingers on the desk. The two detectives looked at each other before completing rock, papers, and scissors. Andrews won and grabbed the file before going around and into the interrogation room.

"We meet again professor." Andrews sat down at the table and watched his lawyer lean over and whisper something in his ear. "Secrets really aren't necessary here."

Montgomery motioned toward his lawyer, "Detective I'd like you to meet Mr. Duncan Marshall, my attorney."

Andrews held out her hand, "Pleased to meet you Mr. Marshall."

"Can we get this started, I have a golf game to get to." Mr. Marshall stated, ignoring her hand, "my client has nothing more to say for the first time he was here."

"Well lucky for your client, we have different questions to ask this time." Andrews opened the file she had in front of her. Pulling out the pictures of all of Worm's victims, she lined them up in front of Dr. Montgomery.

"Are these supposed to mean something to me?" Montgomery looked down at the pictures, "I know all these people because they've been on the news."

Mr. Marshall leaned over and whispered again to his client. "Any questions you have for my client you can address through me."

Andrews leaned back and looked at the glass behind her. Part of her was wishing she could go back a few minutes and lose the rock, paper, and scissors game. "Mr. Marshall, would you please ask your client if he's ever been to 6545 Belle Way, Clarence NY."

Montgomery did show a flash of recognition on his face before looking over at his attorney. Looking back at the detective, "I have not. I know nothing about that address."

"Dr. Montgomery, I would like to inform you that at this moment there is a squad of detectives and crime scene investigators at your house and vacation house. Per the warrant, they are searching through everything. Is there anything you would like to tell us before they call us with an update?"

After receiving a nod from his attorney, he shook his head, "I have nothing to hide. You let me know what you find, if you find anything." Standing up, "I believe we're done here."

Andrews sat still as the two men walked out, she was going to stop him but they had nothing on him, she couldn't hold him. Baker walked into the interrogation room and sat down where Montgomery had been sitting. He arranged the pictures that were on the table into order before putting them into a pile and handing them to Andrews.

"Well, that was a train wreck." Baker smiled at his partner.

Andrews snickered, "Yeah, it really was."

"Nice touch though telling him we were searching the place."

"Didn't work. I have an idea though." She pointed at Baker and nodded. "Yeah, I have an idea."

With that Andrews grabbed everything she had brought in and left the room. Heading back to the conference room, she pulled a rookie officer with her as she walked. "You're with me. I have an assignment for you." Once they got back to the conference room she instructed the officer, "I want you to get me a list. I want to know every single female, well no married too. I want to know every female, male, animal, whatever that Dr. Montgomery has been in contact with professionally, privately, and sexually." She trailed off.

"Andrews, where are you taking this?" Baker was looking at his partner like she was losing it.

"Ok, I know he's known to be a player so the list will be long but if we look at everyone he knows, maybe one of them knows one of the other victims and we can find a connection." Andrews pushed the officer out the door, "Shoo! Get to work, I want a list by the end of the day!"

A few hours later, the officer returned with a list containing what seemed like hundreds of names. Andrews sank into her chair, "I guess I should have expected that, the guy is a professor after all."

"Let me see that list." Baker stole it from her and began crossing off names.

Receiving the list back from Baker, Andrews counted. "Twenty-six. How in the world did you narrow it down?"

"You just need to trust me. A lot of those names were students and other faculty. Of course they would know the next victim because she was also a student there, but they wouldn't know the old man and they wouldn't know the murderer's mother. Plus, look closely at that list again."

Confused, Andrews studied the list. "You can't be serious!"

"See, your hunch was good. Now we have to figure out what they have in common."

Andrews read the names aloud, "Julia Miller, Carson Wayne, and Nancy Holden." She thought for a moment, "Ok, Nancy we knew about but she's dead. Carson makes sense but Julia?"

"Well it could just be that he knew her because she was another student but I didn't see anyone else on the list that we had spoken too when we found Frankie." Baker was feeling excited that this could be a new lead.

"We should get a jump on this. Let's do background checks on all of these and get their recent bank statements and cell phone bills." Andrews went to the front of the station and instructed a few of the rookies on what she needed done for her. "Baker, I have something I need to do but why don't you start looking over the evidence list from the Cullen place."

Baker wasn't sure what she meant by that but it was definitely suspicious. "What does that mean Andrews? What do you have to do that's more important than catching a serial killer?"

"I can't tell you that, but I swear this is important. It may even help." Andrews smiled hopefully and then left the room.

Andrews walked over to the captain's office and sat down. They didn't exchange any words, the captain just picked up the phone and dialed. He told the person on the other line that it was time and then hung up. The two sat there in silence for a while, studying each other's faces. Eventually the captain broke the silence, it was his duty to make sure this was the best decision and he had to be sure he was doing what was right.

"Are you sure you're ready and you want to do this?" He questioned her.

Andrews thought for a moment, "Yes. Let's close the door so we can open the window."

"I had to be sure this is what you wanted." Harris wasn't sure this was the right thing to do but he was going to be certain he ran the mission.

Christopher Rollins walked through the door a moment later. Captain Harris motioned for Andrews to get the blinds and shut the door. As she was closing the door she could see Baker watching, a worried look on his face when he recognized Rollins. She finished closing the door and then sat back down.

"Tell me what the plan is Topher. I want this over with." Andrews was ready, especially if this had something to do with the current case, she needed it done.

"Alright. Here's what we were thinking." The lawyer went through what the DA had come up with and laid out the plan.

An hour later, Andrews was standing alone in an abandoned factory on the East side. She walked a little farther into the main room toward a conveyor of sorts. Behind her she could hear footsteps and she spun around to see three men walking her way. She knew there were snipers up in the rafters but she still couldn't help but feel a little fear.

"Hello?" Andrews called out.

"Hello, hello Ms. Detective. Your friend Corey sends his regards but he's a bit tied up right now. He wishes he could have been here though."

The voice sounded really familiar. Andrews relaxed then when she saw it was her old friend Jasper. He's been undercover in this gang for almost a decade now. Weird fellow but she trusted him. This was for show, he had to keep his cover up. Jasper got in Andrews' face and pulled out a gun. He cocked it and she could feel her heart start to race.

"You're not going to shoot me. It wouldn't be enough to Corey if you just shot me like this." Andrews spoke calmly.

The man laughed and dropped the gun, "No Ms. Detective. I'm not going to shoot you." He leaned in and whispered in her ear, "You are going to die though, but I'm not going to kill you."

At that moment the lights were shut off. Andrews froze in fear from what she was just told and felt someone grab her arm. She pushed away and took off running toward where she remembered the entrance being. Shots rang through the air as Andrews ran. She stumbled over something and fell to the ground. She could see flashes of light coming from the barrels of guns. Something had gone terribly wrong with the plan, someone must have leaked the information. That familiar voice spoke to her again.

"So I lied. I am going to shoot you." Jasper raised the gun and held it directly in front of Andrews.

"No one gave you permission to kill my partner!" Baker screamed at the man before firing his own pistol, shooting Jasper in the chest.

Andrews couldn't move, her body felt frozen. She could feel someone pulling her off the ground and walking her to a corner. She could hear someone talking to her and voices all around but she didn't know what they were saying. She watched the pool of blood grow from around Jasper's body. He was her friend, he was undercover, and he wasn't really a bad man. He tried to kill her, why would he do that? Andrews didn't understand. Jasper was supposed to help, not be the one to take her out.

"Andrews! Can you hear me? Say something if you can hear me!" Baker tried to see any spark in her eyes but saw nothing but fear.

The lights came back on in the factory as armed men swarmed those that were left from Corey's crew. They handcuffed them and sent someone to check the bodies for pulses. There were three down from Corey's team, one of them is Jasper. Rollins came over followed by Captain Harris. Andrews could see them walking toward her, she could hear them asking her questions but she couldn't speak. She just stared at Jasper's body.

Rollins kneeled next to where Baker was holding Andrews, 'I am so sorry. We had no idea that Jasper had turned or I wouldn't have suggested setting this up."

Baker pushed him away, "You're an idiot you know that! You could have gotten her killed with your idiotic plan, you just stay away from her!"

"Andrews, can you hear us?" Captain Harris asked her before waving over one of the medics. "I want you to take her to the hospital to have her looked at. Make sure there's an officer posted by her door, no one and I mean no one except me and the doctors can go in her room." The captain didn't know who to trust at this moment but he wasn't going to take any more chances with her life.

"But sir?" Baker looked at the captain, he didn't understand why he couldn't stay with her.

Harris shook his head, "Baker I need you to stick on this Worm case. After tonight's incident I don't think they're connected."

"Yes, sir." Baker said as he watched the medics put Andrews on a gurney and take her away.

Andrews woke up in the hospital room, she could hear the consistent beep of her heart monitor. "What happened?" She questioned the nurse.

"You had an anxiety attack and went into shock. You're going to be okay, you just need to rest." The nurse informed Andrews.

Andrews leaned back in the bed trying to remember what happened. It all came back to her but in pieces. She remembered Jasper tried to shoot her and that Baker killed Jasper. But how did Baker get there? He wasn't supposed to know. Jasper was supposed to be her friend, why would he want to kill her? She didn't have answers to any of her questions but she did know one thing, she wasn't going to stay another moment in this hospital. People go to hospitals to die, and she wasn't going to die.

Reaching across, Andrews pulled out her IV and pulled the rest of the tubes from her body. She hit the button on the monitor to shut off the machine and then grabbed her clothes. She knew she didn't have long before one of the nurses or doctors came in to check on her and she could already tell through the door's window that she had a detail on her. That left the window.

She looked and saw there was at least a ledge to stand on and a fire escape not too far from her window. She changed out of her robe and then gracefully climbed out the window and made her escape. Knowing there were few she could trust anymore, she made her way over to Baker's house, he was the only one she trusted at this time.

Andrews knocked on the door and smiled when Valerie checked to see who it was. "I'm terribly sorry to show up like this but I need a favor."

Valerie opened the door and motioned for Andrews to come in. "Geoff is very worried about you. They have him off on some sort of tip on his homicide case. He probably won't be home until late."

"Can I please borrow your car?" Andrews decided to be direct, plus where she needed to go was too far to walk. A car was going to be a must.

"Why sure darling" Valerie said, offering Andrews the keys. "Is everything okay dear?"

Andrews hugged the woman, "It will be soon."

With that Andrews took the keys and took off out the door. She got in the car, rolled down the windows, cranked the music and started driving. There was a score to settle and she wasn't going to sleep till this was over, for good this time.

She drove for miles just thinking about her life. It was time to take control back, she was going to show up and go straight to the top. The longer she drove, the more she fumed. Andrews could hear her cell phone constantly ringing on the seat next to her. Every time she would look to check the id. Baker, Harris and Kevin seemed to be taking turns trying to get hold of her. They must have realized she's no longer in the hospital.

A few hundred miles out, she pulled into a gas station and filled up the tank, there were still a few more hours to go. It was almost morning when she got to her destination. Andrews pulled into a dirt driveway and up to an old farm house. She turned off the car and got out, leaving her phone in the car. As she walked up to the house, she reached behind her to check that her gun was tucked safely under her shirt. She wasn't about to take any chances.

Reaching the door, she knocked once. The door swung open and she was greeted by an unshaven man. He smiled at her and held the door open for her to come in. Escorting her toward the back of the house, she was instructed to have a seat out on the patio.

"It's a little early to be making house calls, don't you think?" Another man came out from the house and sat opposite of Andrews. He offered her coffee before taking a sip of his own. "Black right?"

Andrews took the coffee, but set it on the table and didn't touch it again. "I'm not here to be social. I want you to call the heat off on my head. I'm sorry I shot your son, and I'm sorry your other son is an idiot. It's been long enough."

"Well, I agree that Corey is an idiot, and Johnny wanted to be just like his older brother so I guess that would make him an idiot too. They take after their mother." The man leaned back. "I wouldn't be worried about this hit, you have much worse things to be watching out for."

"What do you mean?" Andrews wasn't sure where he was taking this.

Leaning forward, he whispered. "Someone else wants you dead and they are willing to pay an even bigger price, just for the chance to get close to you."

Andrews wondered if this is where the black roses come into play. "Who? Who wants me dead?"

"You'll find out soon enough." He smiled as he leaned back again.

Andrews felt a pinch on her arm and looked over. Junior was sticking a needle in her arm and injecting her with something. She started to sway as things became hazy. Her vision was going out of focus, and then she lost consciousness.

"Welcome home Detective." The man across from her stated. "Sorry it was such a short trip."

Chapter 11: Black Wriggler

"Where am I?" A very groggy Andrews held her head. The room was spinning, causing her to feel dizzy.

Junior handed her a glass of water, "You're safe Bethany."

Andrews sat up and struck the glass away from him. "Don't you touch me!"

"That wasn't very nice of you. I'm trying to be a good host and you don't even say thank you." Junior picked the glass up off the ground and left the room.

Andrews had time to look around at her surroundings. There weren't any windows, only a small vent at the top of the opposite wall, letting in a little light. The only door almost reminded her of a medieval dungeon door. It was almost a relic how it was detailed and designed, with a small window at the top. She was on a cot that seemed brand new, out of some medical equipment catalogue.

She could hear voices through the wall, but couldn't distinguish them. The door opened again and she gasped when she saw who walked through. Their theory had been right. In front of her stood not only Junior but also Dr. Montgomery, Carson and Julia. There was another girl with them but she didn't recognize her.

"Ah, Detective. It's nice of you to join us," Karl Montgomery sneered. "We've been preparing for you."

Andrews tried to wrap her mind around what was taking place. "You've all been helping each other?"

"I'm sure you've heard of strangers on a train, well this is more of strangers with the same blabby therapist." Julia said, distain in her words.

"Nancy was one of you too then?" Andrews questioned.

Montgomery laughed, "She wasn't one of us, and she was weak. That crazy woman had lost her mind and was going to tell you everything."

"We couldn't have her telling our secrets, so I took care of her." Junior finished.

"Yes, we have video of that." Andrews responded.

"Oh good! I hope they put that on the news, that'll make him happy." He seemed quite pleased with himself.

Andrews was confused, "He who?"

Like he got caught with a cookie in his hand, Junior shrunk down. The other glared at him and pushed him out the door. Montgomery stepped up.

"No further questions. Soon enough you'll know everything and then we'll be rid of you as well." He said shutting the door so Junior couldn't come back in.

Julia leaned so she was at eye level with Andrews, "You realize you and your partner have been making it extremely hard for us to accomplish our tasks?"

"Well isn't that a shame? Maybe next time you're trying to kill someone, hide the body better." Andrews hissed back.

Julia swung at Andrews, causing her lip to bleed. "Oops, you might want to take care of that. You wouldn't want a scar on that pretty face."

Andrews tried to stand up to defend herself but the drugs made her so weak, she was still really dizzy and fell to the floor. Those in the room took turns kicking her and punching her in the face. She curled into a ball to try and protect herself the best she could. She hoped they'd just finish her off the pain was too much.

Montgomery called the attack off and everyone stepped back. "Sleep tight Detective, you have a big day in front of you tomorrow." Montgomery whispered as they all left Andrew's alone.

Sounded exciting. Andrews blamed herself for being in this situation and now no one would know where she was because she didn't answer any of their calls. Not that it would help, she didn't even know where she was or what state she was in. Last she remembered she was back in Boyertown visiting Corey's father, which was another stupid mistake. Thinking first really wasn't her strength but at least she knew the theory she and Baker came up with was the correct one. Now how to go about putting them behind bars and getting her out of this room.

She thought about her favorite movie Kiss the Girls again and how Ashley Judd's character escapes. Plausible, she too has kickboxing training but which one could she lure back in and take advantage of? That young girl seemed a possibility or even Junior. No that probably wouldn't work, so what would Nancy Drew do? Well, Nancy wouldn't have been dumb enough to get caught in this situation and she would have been written out of the situation in two pages if she was the one trapped. Andrews knew she was alone and didn't have any help coming this time. No partner to take the bullet for her or uncle to send her away to keep her safe. She was completely alone.

Andrews tried to stand again but discovered she was still too groggy and could barely move without getting dizzy and having to sit back down. Junior must have injected her with some sort of a tranquilizer. Giving up, she laid down on the bed and worked on just trying to get the room to stop spinning. Even her hangovers in the past hadn't been this bad. Her body was aching in pain, her ribs bruised and blood was dripping from somewhere. She tried to stop the bleeding where she could and treat herself, eventually giving up and just laying down on the cot.

Keeping time was impossible but what felt like eternity, the young girl came back with a plate full of food. Andrews sat up ready for another attack, and just watched the girl as she sat it on the bed next to her. She seemed to be in her late teens or early twenties. Blonde hair, extremely tall for a girl so she probably is an athlete of some type. She was the one Andrews hadn't recognized though that didn't stop the girl from helping in beating the crap out of her earlier.

"What's your name?" Andrews asked the girl.

She shyly replied, never making eye contact. "They told me not to talk to you."

"I'm not going to hurt you, I just wanted to know your name."

"It's Kelly." The girl said finally looking up. "I'm not like them."

Andrews nodded, "I know sweetie. Do you know what they've each done?"

"Yes. I was in their group when they planned it all and he told them what to do."

There was that he again, but who was he? "Their therapy group right?"

The girl just nodded. "I really shouldn't be talking to you."

"I don't want to eat alone, couldn't you stay for just a little longer? We don't have to talk?" Andrews was going to make friends with this girl and try to get her to help her escape.

"That would be okay. I have some time before it's my turn." The girl noted, "I had to wait till last because mine's the hardest."

"Yours?"

Kelly continued, "My mark. Karl had his girlfriend, Julia had her forbidden lover, Carson his father, and Junior has you. I'm next."

"I thought you said you weren't like them." Andrews was starting to think this girl was worse than all of them. She seemed innocent a moment ago.

"I'm not. I'm not going to listen to him, my boyfriend deserves much worse than what he told me to do." Kelly smiled thinking about what she had planned.

Andrews sat back from the girl scared to ask anything else. "What does your boyfriend deserve if I may ask?"

"Well see I caught him cheating on me, so I'm going to kill him. Very slowly and probably painfully. I don't just want to strangle him, that's not as much fun." The girl stood. "Well I need to go, he's going to be here soon and I have to get my jar. Enjoy your dinner."

There were no words, Andrews just waved and put her fork down. There was something seriously wrong with that little girl. Andrews wondered just what kind of group therapy session was taking place if this is what came of that. She always thought therapy was supposed to help people but if this is what occurred then she really didn't want to ever go to therapy herself.

The girl had left the little window on the door open when she left. Andrews could hear voices coming from the other room. Maybe if she listened, she'd be able to tell who this he was they all kept talking about. There were a lot more voices than she recognized. Definitely more than the five that had been in her room earlier. Did this mean there were more bodies out there? Andrews tried to stop thinking of the worst and just paid attention to what was taking place around her.

The voices were muffled but it sounded like a party almost. They were all happy, sharing their stories of how they killed, feeding off the other's stories. Andrews was getting worried they'd work themselves up and go have a killing spree. She could hear the other door open, it creaked and echoed through the room. Then she realized, it echoed because the room was silent now. She heard nothing. No, footsteps. She could hear footsteps walking around and whispers as they passed.

"My friends, thank you for gathering here together tonight." A new voice called out. "Please do not stop the party on my account. We have much to celebrate tonight."

The noise level rose again and Andrews could no longer distinguish between them. That voice though, she knew that voice but couldn't place it. She's met a lot of people though between two states so it could really be anyone. For now she'd let it go and focus on trying to hear what they were all saying. Andrews listened for a few more moments before the voices stopped again.

Junior spoke, "Kelly, is Kelly still here? Can you please come over here?" He paused, "Ah, yes. Kelly I would like to present you with your jar. When you reach the point of the kill, stun your victim, place the sacrifice into their mouth and one in the hand. Let him know how he makes you feel hated and hasn't loved you."

"I will. Thank you so much for this opportunity." Kelly squealed excitedly.

"Be careful my friend, remember to not get caught and not leave any evidence for them to find. If you are caught, you do not know me. You do not know of this group, or you too will be a sacrifice." The unknown man voiced.

"Yes master." Kelly humbly spoke, "I will make you proud."

Andrews was confused, did she just enter the Twilight Zone and get captured by a cult? They were tracking a serial killer but this was much more than that. They were using sacrifices for something and being controlled by this man. Andrews figured he must have something over them, blackmail. The party started back up again and went all night. It took all she could muster to stay awake till the party was over and most of the guests had left.

The noise level had died down enough for Andrews to hear the conversations again. They were all arguing what to do about her. She could hear Montgomery trying to convince the others just to dispose of her, they didn't need her. Junior didn't want to though and since she was his, he got the final say. He apparently hadn't received his jar yet and he wanted to wait till the master approved of his kill so he could join him.

That would mean that Kelly wouldn't be the last, Junior would be. Maybe it was one of the others, Andrews wasn't sure but she knew she definitely had to get out of this place. She heard them discuss who would stay behind and watch her. Julia offered to take the first shift and the rest left. Andrews decided this was her chance. She'd get Julia to come in and she'd knock her out and run.

Julia came into the room shortly after holding a gun at Andrews. "Junior didn't have the guts to kill you, but I do."

"You don't want to do that though, then Junior doesn't get his sacrifice. Your master wouldn't be happy if you took that away from him."

"I don't care." Julia aimed the gun at Andrews and squeezed the trigger.

Andrews could feel the blood drain from her face. She felt cold and wanted to collapse. Then she noticed Julia fumbling with the gun, angry. Andrews looked down and noticed nothing new was bleeding, nothing hurt like a gunshot wound would. She wasn't shot, she was in pain but she wasn't shot. Andrews wasn't sure if there'd be another chance so she used all her strength and stood up, punching Julia in the face causing her to fall. Bending down, Andrews grabbed the gun off the floor and laughed.

"You idiot, you still have the safety on." Andrews took the safety off and shot Julia in the leg. "Didn't your master ever teach you to use a gun?"

192

"You bitch! He'll get you for this! He will find you!" Julia screamed grabbing at her wound.

Andrews walked over to the door, still holding the gun, "Tell him I'm waiting. Whenever he's ready to finish this, he can come find me."

Julia snickered, "Oh he'll find you and you'll wish you didn't say that." She watched as Andrews walked out the door, "He will find you!" She screamed.

Andrews found herself in a giant room, no furniture of any kind. It appeared to be almost like a ballroom. She saw there were two doors, one had to lead out. Which one though? Andrews tried the first door on the right and gasped once she saw the contents. That door definitely did not lead outside.

"What is wrong with these people?" Andrews whispered to herself.

She looked around the room. The walls had been divided up into sections. She hobbled inside and saw the room opened up and was actually a long hallway. Each sections on the walls had pictures of a different person and she could only assume the murderer's name above them. She saw Leah's pictures with Karl's name. There was even a picture of Leah's cold corpse and what seemed to be a shot with Julia and Karl smiling with the body.

There were definitely more sections and more pictures and names than Andrews had counted on. Those that had finished the deed all had pictures with the dead body. Andrews found her column with Junior's name. They were pictures from a long time ago and also from the past week with Kevin. She tried to remember if she had known Junior from Boyertown but couldn't place him. She didn't know what she had done to him to make him want to kill her.

Andrews knew she couldn't spend any more time looking through the room, she had to get out of there. She grabbed a few of the pictures as she went back through the room. Leaving she went over to the other door and opened it. Finally, fresh air blew onto her face. She saw Julia's car sitting right outside the door and went to see if it was unlocked. Of course not, this wasn't the movies and that would be too easy. She thought about breaking the window but hot wiring a car was not something she learned growing up so keys were going to be a must.

Walking back into the dungeon area of the house, Andrews found Julia still holding her wound and trying to mess with her phone. Andrews took the phone away and saw Julia had bloodied up the screen too much to do anything, so she pocketed the phone and pointed the gun once again at Julia.

"Ok, Julia. Where are the keys to your car? I will shoot your other leg." Andrews threatened.

"I'll never tell you!" Julia spat back at her. "You look like hell by the way."

Andrews leaned down and pushed Julia over and searched her pockets. "Fine, be difficult. I really don't care at this point. And remind me to thank you and your friends later for my new look." She pulled the keys from Julia's jacket, "And just so you know, I found your little secret room with all the pictures. That'll help the DA out a lot when trying to get the jury to sentence you to death. I'll make sure I'm front row for your execution."

"You won't be able to stop us. He's much smarter than anyone gives him credit for."

Andrews rolled her eyes, "I'm so sick of you all worshipping this freak. He's human, he really can't be all that special. Messed up in the head sure, I see that. He'll bleed just the same as you when I find him. That I can promise you."

"Not if he kills you first." Julia hissed.

"You're obnoxious, just shut up already." Andrews kicked Julia in the face, causing her to become unconscious. "And that's for breaking my nose first."

Andrews left the house and got into Julia's car and started the engine. Pulling the phone she took out of her pocket, she cleaned off the screen and dialed Baker's number. It went straight to voicemail so she left him a message, telling him she was okay and coming into the station. She checked the GPS on the phone and then added where she was and that the local police should be sent to put a perimeter around the house. Then she hung up and started driving.

Baker called back a moment later, "I got your message; we were worried you were dead. Where are you? Are you okay?"

"I'm fine. Just got a little lost for a while but I'm okay. You need to send police to the address I gave you in the voicemail. It's a meeting house for Worm's followers and I left a little present for when they get here." Andrews caught him up.

"We're just glad you're alive. We went to the hospital to check on you and you were gone." Baker still sounded really worried. "Do you remember who took you?"

Andrews laughed, "Took me? You think someone kidnapped me?" She pulled over the car, the drugs were still in her system and she couldn't talk and drive at the same time right now. The car was swerving a bit much for her likes. "No one took me Baker, I went out the window and ran off."

"You climbed out the window! Are you crazy?" Baker yelled.

She could hear someone in the background having some sort of meltdown. "Baker, I'm fine. I'll be back in a few hours. I'm just outside the New York state line."

"You come straight to the station, do you hear me? You have a lot of explaining to do and we need to fill you in on the case." Baker's voice got calm and quiet, "There's been another body found and we think there could be at least ten more that we have yet to find."

Andrews wondered if the newest victim could be Kelly's doing. "Ok. I'll be right in. Just have one little stop to make first."

"Andrews don't you -"Baker got cut off.

She had hung up the phone before he could finish his sentence. She knew what he'd say, to be safe and not do something stupid. Had he knew what she'd been through, he'd know the time for being stupid was long past. Now it's time to get a little revenge and put those crazy therapy groupies in jail.

Andrews drove to the address they had found for Carson Wayne. She knew he'd still probably be at home because he would never expect her to escape and tell someone what he had done. The cops sure weren't going to call him on such little evidence. He'd feel safe and so he'd probably be in bed with his wife not worried at all.

Andrews pulled into his driveway and checked how many bullets she had in the clip before cocking the pistol and getting out of the car. She walked up to the door and rang the bell. Carson opened the door and quickly tried to shut it, fear flashing in his eyes. Andrews had stuck her foot in the door before he could close it and she pushed her way in. Holding the gun to his head she pushed him into the den area and onto a chair. His wife had come down the stairs and Andrews redirected the gun toward her.

"You need to have a seat ma'am and listen to what your husband has to say." Turning back to Carson, Andrews once again held the gun at his head. "Would you like to tell your wife what you did or should I?"

"Please don't. I didn't do anything wrong," Carson pleaded.

Carson's wife started to cry, "What is she talking about? Why does she have a gun?"

He looked over at his wife, "She's crazy. She's the one that killed your father. Now she wants to kill us."

"You snake! Tell her the truth or I will!" Andrews was angry now. How dare he try and pin the murder on her. Sure, she was a little off her rocker right now but felt she had every right to be.

"I told her, I told her you killed him! It's the truth, please don't hurt us." Carson put his hands up to protect himself, as he quivered in his chair.

Andrews laughed, "Fine. I'll tell her." She turned to his wife. "Your husband threw your father into the garbage compactor where your father lived. He killed him for his money because someone in some cult he met in therapy told him too."

"Carson," his wife said between sobs, "Carson what is she talking about?"

"Don't listen to her honey, she's crazy. I didn't do anything to Charlie, I wouldn't hurt him. You know that."

"Really?" Andrews pulled one of the pictures she had taken out of her pocket. "Here's a nice shot of you and Charlie right before you threw him into the compactor." Andrews looked at the picture once more before handing it to his wife.

Carson stood from the chair, pushing Andrews down and running toward the door. Andrews fired a shot off and hit Carson in the foot, causing him to drop to the ground. She stood up and walked over to where he was laying on the floor.

"You're very lucky that was just your foot. I thought about killing you but where would the fun be in that." Andrews turned back to his wife, "I'm going to be on my way now. You two enjoy your evening. I'm sure you have a lot to talk about."

When she got back to the car, Andrews dialed 911 and left a tip that she heard gunshots and believe there was a domestic dispute taking place at that address. She told the cops to hurry that it sounded like the couple was going to kill each other. With that she put the phone on the seat next to her and pulled out of the driveway. Part of her felt a little evil for what she did, but he had it coming and his wife deserved to know. Sure, she could lose her badge for this, but she didn't really care at the moment, she was on a mission.

Andrews debated just going back to the station and giving up on her mission. The thought fleeted from her mind as fast as it had come to her. This was something she needed to do before they took her badge from her. Next stop was to see the professor. Andrews cranked up the music and sped off.

A couple of hours later, Andrews pulled onto the Buffalo campus and headed for the professor's office. She could tell people were staring at her, but she didn't care, let them stare. A little blood wasn't going to kill her and she had to fight through the pain a little longer, just long enough to finish what they had started.

Andrews knocked on the professor's door and opened when she heard a voice responding to come in. She quickly opened the door, stepped inside and shut it behind her. Karl Montgomery looked up from his desk and at first seemed worried, then he leaned back in his chair and folding his hands smiling to himself.

"I see you've escaped." Montgomery noted.

Andrews pulled the gun from her shirt and aimed for his head. "I see you're still an asshole with a superiority complex."

"Touché detective." He sat up in his chair, "What exactly are you planning on doing with that gun?"

"Did you really think it was fair to have it four against one earlier? Especially considering the one was drugged? Did you really think that I wouldn't get out and hunt you down to expose you as the fraud you are?" Andrews sat in the seat opposite Montgomery.

"What is your terms detective?"

Andrews laughed, "You think I have terms. You killed a girl for who knows what reason, you beat up a detective, oh and can't forget the kidnapping part. You have some secret cult you're in that is planning to murder a lot more people and you're asking for terms?" She leaned forward, "I'm sorry professor, but there won't be any plea bargains anymore, I'll see to it personally."

Montgomery stood by his desk, "Unless you're actually going to do something with that gun or have a warrant I'm going to have to ask you to leave. I have a lot of papers I need to grade yet, see I was a little busy earlier and couldn't get to them."

"Wrong thing to say buddy." Andrews aimed the gun and shot Montgomery in the left shoulder.

He looked stunned that she had actually pulled the trigger. Slumping back down into his chair, Montgomery reached for the phone. Andrews knocked it off the desk and held the gun out again.

"Nice try." Andrews pulled the phone out still holding the gun to the professor and dialed 911 again. "Yes, I'd like to report gunshots on the college campus. I saw someone run from the faculty building holding a gun and waving it in the air, I think they shot one of the professors." She made her voice seem frantic and then hung up the phone. "Good day professor, you might want to rest up. You will have a very busy day tomorrow."

"You won't get away with this! I'll tell them you're the one that shot me." Montgomery threatened.

"Be my guest." Andrews responded as she left his office, closing the door behind her.

She had to admit to herself, she was starting to feel a little better. There was really only one person left on her list, well, besides Junior and whoever this Worm person was. Andrews figured the other body, they had already found must have been Kelly's ex-boyfriend so where would Kelly go. She really had no idea, but she did know that going back to the station would mean back to the hospital.

Andrews knew of somewhere she could go to get cleaned up and not be tattled on. That would be her next stop. Thankfully, this friend of hers was not far from the campus and it wasn't long before she was knocking on another door. A middle age woman opened the door and after seeing it was Andrews, immediately opened the door and let her in. The woman checked outside before shutting the door and locking three deadbolts.

"I'm so sorry to intrude like this, but I need some help." Andrews began. "I'm in a bit of trouble."

"Now, I won't ask questions if you'll sit down and let me clean you up." The woman demanded of Andrews. "I'm guessing the other guy looks a lot worse than you do."

"Thank you Kim. I wouldn't have come if it wasn't an emergency." Andrews took a seat and waited for the woman to come back from collecting supplies. "And they actually don't, not yet anyways."

Kim came back into the room and started cleaning the blood of Andrews' face. "Anytime. We help each other, that's how it's always been. Something seems different though."

"Let's just say I took control of my life for once. I'm tired of everyone else making decisions for me." Andrews sighed, "I may have gone to the dark side as well, but I'm discovering it's more fun on this side."

"That's a slippery slope, just be careful to slide down it slowly." Kim reminded her.

Andrews flinched as Kim applied disinfectant to the wounds. She finished cleaning up the wounds and then put a band aid over the cut on Andrew's forehead. "I'm not sure what I can do about the broken nose and bruised ribs, but you're at least not going to bleed out."

"It's okay, I appreciate the help. I just need to be able to get around a little while longer and then I can go get checked out at a hospital." Andrews commented.

"Is there anything I can help you with? I can use a few of my contacts and try to find something out if you'd like?" Kim offered.

Andrews stood from the couch, "I appreciate the offer, but I wouldn't want to put you in the position. This is a little different than coming to you for information on a theft or dealer." She would feel awful if something happened to this lady, she's been a helpful source for years.

"Well the offer stands if you change your mind." Kim too stood and led Andrews back to the door. "Is there anything else you need before you head out and do things I probably shouldn't know about?" She smiled knowingly at Andrews.

"I'm good, but thank you for all your help." Andrews stated after giving Kim a hug and leaving.

Andrews got back in the car and headed for the station. She knew she was going to have to listen to a few lectures and probably be reprimanded for her later decisions, but she wanted it over sooner rather than later. The drive there took faster than she expected. Andrews took a deep breath after she parked and got out of the car.

"Ready or not, let's get arrested." Andrews said, walking toward the station.

Chapter 12: Field Worm

She walked through the door of the station and noticed immediately, she was again in a fishbowl. The receptionist picked up the phone and dialed someone letting them know Andrews was back. As she started walking down the hallway, she could see Baker coming toward her. When he got to her, he grabbed her arm and pulled her into the first empty conference room, shutting the door behind them.

"Do you realize you've been named as the person running around shooting suspects?" Baker accused Andrews, "Please tell me that wasn't you." He looked her over and then asked, "What happened to you?"

"Nice of you to care." Andrews hissed. "Well, where should I start? I was kidnapped, beat up in a very unfair fight, drugged, shot at and pretty much left in a dungeon awaiting my death."

Baker had a pained look on his face, "Well I'm sorry. Why did you run though? Where did you go?" He started pacing, "They have a warrant out for your arrest. The captain is beside himself and getting frequent calls from your uncle."

"I got it, I'm being grounded." Andrews sat down at the conference table. "I'll stay here while you run off and get daddy."

"Look, I don't know what happened to you, but the attitude isn't going to help your case. You may want to reconsider how you handle this before the captain gets in here." Baker warned her before leaving.

Andrews sat there thinking for a moment before grabbing at one of the notebooks and a pen. She left a note for Baker and the captain about the location she was held and that there was someone pulling the strings that they hadn't known about before. There was no way she was going to sit around to be lectured and then thrown in jail because they didn't understand the situation.

She put the pad of paper so it faced the door of the conference room and took her leave. The receptionist tried to stop Andrews but couldn't catch her in time. Andrews got back in Julia's car and started driving away. She could see Baker and the captain running out the front doors, chasing her down. Then she saw Kevin just standing there watching her. She knew they were going to radio in that she was on the run. Andrews knew she'd be in a lot more trouble if she got caught now. She needed to finish this though and they wouldn't understand.

They'd be looking for her and hopefully didn't get the plates off the car just make and model. She'd have to stash it for a while and maybe get a new vehicle later one. That wasn't something she needed to worry about right now. Currently the only thing on her mind was somewhere to go hide. She needed a safe place to lay low for a day or so.

Andrews didn't want to drag Kim farther into this so there was somewhere else she'd have to go. First things first, she needed to drop by the apartment and get Bailey. She knew Kevin probably took care of her while she was being held prisoner. She needed a friend right now though, and that dog was all she had. There was a back entrance into the apartment complex where she could enter without the squad cars out front noticing. She made sure she knew of all exits when she moved in in case, Corey sent his goons after her.

Pulling into the back alley, Andrews got out of the car and climbed the fire escape and entered the back door. She got to her apartment and went in to find Perez sitting, watching TV. Right now she really wished she could have left the dog, but knew that would have never happened.

205

"Welcome home killer. Come to pick something up?" Perez questioned getting up from the couch, gun drawn and pointed at Andrews. "Please do not make me shoot you."

Andrews greeted her dog, "I'm here for Bailey and I'm not a killer."

"You pretty much threw that son-in-law of the human compactor waste to the dogs. His wife shot and killed him after your little visitor."

"Oh really." Andrews smiled, "What visit though, I was kidnapped remember?"

Perez moved closer, "Sure you were. There are witnesses who have seen you all over the city tonight. I was told if you showed up to bring you in, even if it meant giving you a new scar."

"Survived one gunshot already, I think I could survive another." Andrews dared.

Andrews moved slowly around the apartment, keeping an eye on Perez. She got together Bailey's things and put her leash on. Then she went about the apartment filling a bag of clothes and her notes on the case. Perez didn't try and stop her though he stood there and followed her with his gun as she packed. Once she finished she went over to the door and grabbed Bailey's leash.

"If you're going to shoot me you need to do it now." Andrews informed him as she opened the door.

"I was never going to shoot you, I just want to be able to tell the captain, I held you at gun point the entire time and you escaped me." Perez lowered his weapon. "Good luck out there."

"Thanks." She responded as she left with her puppy. "Oh and when you do finally call into the station, please apologize for me. I have to do this on my own, I hope you understand."

"No need to tell me Andrews." Perez laughed, "You're wild and crazy but that's what make you, you. Baker and I have your back."

'Thanks," She said again before slipping out into the hall and retracing her steps to the back alley.

Andrews had another contact she could crash with till she solved this case. She was more worried about who the Worm gang would send for her than she was about the police catching up. Hopefully Baker would read her note and convince the squad to stop searching for her and work on the case as well. With how many voices she heard that night and the walls lined with pictures, this was going to get a lot worse before it got any better.

She pulled up to a house that sat back from the road. It had a nice wrap around porch and shutters. Seemed a little too picturesque for Andrews to be hiding out in but she didn't know of anywhere else to go. Andrews rang the doorbell and was greeted by an older lady. The face seemed familiar and sparked memories. The woman had aged a little since the last time she'd seen her. There were a few more wrinkles around her eyes.

"Bethany, to what do I owe the pleasure?" The older woman asked.

"I need a place to stay for a little while." Andrews loathed this woman and didn't trust her but she was desperate. "Can I please stay here for a few days Loretta?" She hoped the woman didn't hold the same grudge and would let her in.

"Call me Grandma and you can stay as long as you wish." Loretta opened the door, allowing Bethany to come in. "And who is this?" She gestured toward the puppy.

Bethany undid the leash, "This is Bailey, and she'll be staying too. And I won't be calling you that, I'll only be here a few days at the most."

Bethany led Bailey into the house and then followed herself. She watched as Loretta closed the door behind them. Bethany noticed there were pictures on the front wall and went over to look.

"Suit yourself. You can have your old room, I'm sure you remember where it is." Loretta instructed before disappearing into the living room.

"Ok Bailey, let's go upstairs." Bethany grabbed her stuff from the car and carried it upstairs to her old room, from when she'd stay the summers with her grandmother. That was a long time ago before her dad had passed away. Things had changed shortly after though and even with knowing Loretta lived a few blocks away, Bethany never visited. She couldn't stomach seeing the woman who ruined her life.

Walking into her old room was like walking into a museum. Nothing had changed, it looked like it had been dusted recently and the bed sheets changed. She just put everything down and unpacked what she had brought along on the case. Grabbing tape from her bag, she started hanging pictures on the wall and adding sticky notes with what she remembered from the house she had been prisoner in.

The only way she would be able to stay ahead of Worm would be to get to these others from the therapy group before they could complete their kills. She'd have to be on the lookout for Junior too and make sure she didn't end up on the victim list. First thing in the morning she would ask around and try to find out where their group therapy session took place. Maybe that way she'd be able to get a list of names.

Bethany finished putting together her map of events that had occurred during this Worm case. Since being kidnapped and her moment flirting with the dark side, a few things were starting to make more sense. The therapy group was definitely at the center of all this but how it got started, Bee wasn't sure. Not yet anyways. If each member of the therapy group picked a person that had hurt them as their target, then why would the puppet master care if those people died or not. One man couldn't possibly gain anything from having a bunch of strangers kill people who wronged them.

"I laid out some snacks if you're feeling hungry" A voice from the other side of the door called out.

Bee went over to the door and opened it a crack, "Thank you, Loretta but I'm fine for now."

The woman shrugged, "well it's there if you change your mind."

Closing the door, Bethany went back to her board. She knew it would be there later. Right now though she needed to rest, being kidnapped and going after a bunch of suspects puts a toll on a girl. A few hour nap would probably do her good right now. She'll start looking for leads on the therapy group once she wakes up. Locking the door and sticking her gun under her pillow, Bethany laid down and tried to relax. She noticed Bailey had already made herself comfortable and was also napping. It wasn't long before Bethany drifted off and fell asleep.

The sound of sirens and car doors slamming woke Bee abruptly from her nap. She should have known they'd find her fast. Bethany did her best to grab what she had put up on the wall and stuff it back into her bag. She took what else she could and slowly opened the door ready to sneak out into the hallway. She could hear Loretta talking to the officers below, claiming not to have seen Bethany since she was a girl. The officers asked her to give them a call if anything changes and then they left.

Bethany walked over to Loretta and caught Bailey wandering along behind. She reached over and scratched Bailey's ear. "What did they want?" She asked Loretta.

"Don't' worry about it, I told them I hadn't seen you." Loretta mentioned. "Oh, and I drove the car around back into the barn. Figured you wouldn't want anyone to see it."

Bethany had to give the woman credit, she was quick on her feet. Must be a genetic thing. Bethany sat down on the couch and coaxed Bailey up with her to hold. Loretta sat in the chair opposite Bethany. The two women sat in silence, they were content with not talking. Considering their past, there wasn't much to talk about anyways.

"Your mother called me a few months back, said you just vanished." Loretta watched Bethany's face. "She wanted to know if I had seen you."

"And, what did you tell her?"

Loretta stood, "You want some tea, and I'll get some." She walked over into the kitchen, "I told her the truth. I hadn't seen you since the funeral."

Bethany got up and followed the woman into the kitchen, "Look, I'm sorry for how you've been treated since dad died. You lied to us though."

"I didn't lie, I chose not to tell you the truth about him. It was to protect you."

"You had no right! You should have told us what he was into." Bethany sat down at the dining table. "We could have prepared ourselves at least."

Loretta poured tea into two cups and joined Bethany at the table. "Your father was always a curious boy growing up. He needed to be involved in everything and," she paused, "eventually that came back to haunt him. He got in with the wrong people who cost him his life."

"You hurt my family though." Bethany played with the tea cup, "you told us he had run off with another woman. Do you know what that did to my mother?"

"It was easier than the truth." Loretta's voice grew, "Did you want me to tell you that your father was a murderer? He was an evil man Bethany. There was something dark in him since he was little. I saw it the whole time." Her voice dropped to normal again, "I thought maybe if he got married and started a family he'd straighten himself out."

"You thought wrong. You should have warned us." Bethany got up and put her cup in the sink. She stood there, unable to move.

"You're his daughter, I see him in you." Loretta stood, "I needed to protect you like I couldn't him. And now look at you, following in your father's footsteps. Shooting at random people and running from the cops."

"I am not my father!" Bethany turned and screamed at her grandmother. "The only thing I've done wrong is come here." She stormed off into the living room. "I'm leaving Bailey with you, I have unfinished business to take care of."

"I'll take care of her for you." Loretta whispered. She knew this girl was just as stubborn as her father, there was no use begging her to stay.

"Thanks." Bethany nodded before heading back to the bedroom to collect her stuff.

She gathered what she could and went around back to the barn. After loading up the car, she decided to make a quick phone call.

"Hey Baker, don't hang up and don't say my name." Bethany warned, "I'm heading over to where they kept me prisoner. Can you meet me there? Alone preferably."

Hanging up she put down the phone and started the car. Bethany drove back over to where she had been held. There was already crime scene tape around the perimeter of the house, so most of the evidence was probably gone. She saw Baker's car out front with no one inside. She figured he must already be in the house.

Bethany parked the car a block away and took off for the back of the house. She peered in the window and noticed Baker standing there. Sneaking around back she slipped through the door. Bethany walked over to where Baker was and waited in the doorway.

"Did you manage to come alone?" She questioned her partner.

"Yeah but not for long, they'll be back anytime now." Baker's looked worn. "So what have you been up to lately?"

Bethany smiled, "Oh you know, the usual. Shooting people, running from the cops."

"That's not funny. What is going on with you Andrews?" Baker grew stern.

"Look, let's not argue. We're here to search the house."

"The department already took most of the stuff here for evidence. The pictures are all gone." Baker motioned to the wall behind them.

Bethany shook her head, "I don't care about the pictures. What I came for is over in the room they kept me tied up."

"Lead on," he motioned with his hand.

They walked through the house to the back room, Bethany felt herself remembering the fear of being trapped there. That was definitely something she wouldn't want to experience ever again. She looked around the room trying to remember where she heard the noises.

"What are we looking for?" Baker questioned.

"I'm not sure. I remember hearing noises coming from behind me, and clearly the only thing behind this chair bolted on the ground is a wall." Bethany moved over to the back wall. "I'm thinking it's a false wall and we're going to find something important behind it."

Baker started tapping on the wall, trying to hear for a hollow area. Finally found one and faced Bethany pointing at the area. They both located objects and hacked away at the drywall. Eventually there was a hole big enough for them to fit through into the next room. They stood there staring at what decorated the room, unable to process this new information.

One of the walls had shelving units littered with jars. They each seemed to be filled with a different colored dirt. Books were stacked along the bottom shelf that looked worn and tattered. The titles read of different entomology books, seeming to specialize in annelids. The opposite wall had weapons hanging from it; ropes, guns, wires, and pipes. Apparently the mission, whatever it was for these people was not over.

"Andrews, what exactly happened while you were here?" Baker asked.

She couldn't answer him, sirens were coming from a distance. "I got to get out of here." Bethany took off for the back door. She stopped and turned to face Baker, "Hey, you should check out the therapy groups around here."

"Yeah, why's that?"

"That's how this whole mess got started. They're all from the same group." She smiled, "I'll be in touch."

Baker waved, "Just be safe out there. Stop shooting people would you? You're giving me a bad name."

"Anything for you partner!" And with that she was gone, running back toward the car.

Bethany sat in her car for a while, watching the action take place a block away. They brought box after box out and loaded them into a truck. Bethany sat there for an hour watching the process. She caught sight of Baker leaving with another cop in his car, and followed after him. She really hoped he was following up her tip about the therapy session. Making sure to keep out of sight of the commotion Bethany followed Baker's car all the way to a building outside of town.

She parked around the side of the building and watched them go in. Debating whether to go in or not, she decided to stay in the car. Bethany watched the front door, there were people constantly coming and going from that place. She decided to drive around the building and see if she could find anything. The sign out front read that it was a community center. Bethany was confused how a murderous cult could be working out of a community center. Bethany parked when she saw Baker and his new partner coming out of the building.

Bethany caught Baker's glance and she walked over to her car. She rolled down the window so she could talk to him. "You find out anything?"

"Yeah, we got a list of names of the different support groups. Saw Montgomery's name on one of the lists." Baker showed her what they found.

"That's where you start then." Andrews took a look and then handed it back. "What did you tell your partner?"

Baker laughed, "I told him my sister was meeting me here to drop something off."

"Ok, well here. Take some of my notes back with you, said I ran from your place and grabbed them for you." Andrews handed them over. "Thank for not treating me like a felon Geoff, I appreciate you trusting me."

"Oh, you're a loaded cannon just waiting to go off, I'm more scared of getting in your way." He smiled before walked back over to his car.

With the therapy group being handled, Bethany was free to start a hunt of her own. She was going after the person targeting her before he could finish the job he started. Now, if a crazy rookie murdering cop were to hide out, where would that place be? Bethany thought of an abandoned factor she knew down past East Amherst Street. It was over by the university, she had remembered seeing it while they were investigating Frankie's murder. That would be a great place to have a secret hideout.

Bethany drove to the other side of town and starting scanning for where she remembered the factory being. She pulled over quite a distance and noticed the gate had been pushed open a little. Figures this would all go down here, just like in a horror movie. Bethany got out of the car and fit as many weapons as she could on her person.

Carefully, she walked over to the gate and slipped through. She tried to stay on the outskirts of the parking lot to stay out of sight of anyone keeping watch. Bethany found an area covered in shrubs and decided to settle in there until it got dark. That gave her time to think of her plan when really all it did was give her time to get worked up.

A few hours later dusk had settled in and she was beyond pissed at Junior. She was ready to go in there and take him out. Slowly she made her way up to the building and around to the side door. She tried the handle, it fell out into her hand. Looking down, she snickered, a broken door, go figure. Bethany entered quietly and looked around, gun out in front of her. She could hear muffled voices but didn't see any movement.

She walked around to the back of the factory, ducking between the conveyor belts. The voices got louder, but they were above her. There must have been an office up there. She stayed silent, trying to distinguish just how many voices there were. She knew she was a good shot, but she wasn't superhuman, there was no way she could take them all on herself. Two of the voices she knew, one was definitely Junior and the other was a voice from the other night. She recognized it but couldn't put a name to it. Unfortunately, it wasn't the leader that would have been way too easy. Now was her shot. She'd have to make her way up the stairs, over to the office and catch them off guard. Sounded great in her head, but to actually pull it off would be a different story.

She had a moment where she thought about just blowing the entire place up and killing everyone inside. That was probably a bit much though, she didn't need anyone else's blood on her hands like she had Carson's now. Bethany knew when she'd leave his wife would kill him and yet she didn't do her duty and try and stop her. Part of her wanted him dead so there was no sympathy. Just like the two voices she heard now. They kidnapped her and tortured her, Junior even wanted to kill her. Why would she want to let them get arrested and thrown in jail? They'd probably take a plea and be out on the streets in no time.

That was too good for them and she wouldn't allow it. That's why she needed to do this alone, somehow she was going to get up to the office and end this now. Bethany remembers what Loretta had told her about being like her father. Everyone has a little dark in them though, that wasn't something just in her. So yeah, she was flirting with the idea of being dark more than she had in the past but times had changed. She's being hunted for heaven's sake, doesn't that give her any sort of right to kill if necessary.

Bethany was lost in her train of thought and didn't notice the voices getting closer. Someone had come down the stairs and was headed in her direction. She didn't notice, just kept her back to the wall, crouched, still debating what her next move should be. The steps got closer and then there was a click.

"Well, hello detective. I've been waiting for you." Junior held the gun in front of Bethany's face.

Chapter 13: Garden Worm

"Why don't you come with me?" Junior stated, gun still pointed at her.

Bethany stood, "If you're giving me the option I'd have to decline, I think we've bonded enough recently don't you?"

Junior waved the gun, "Let's go."

"OK, suit yourself." Bethany started to walk. "More bonding time it is," she mumbled under her breath.

They walked over to the steps. Junior nudged her with the gun to continue walking. Slowly Bethany started up the stairs while keeping an eye on her surroundings. Still seemed like there were only two of them. Junior and that voice she had heard before. They reached the office where Bethany was directed to sit in a chair. Junior tied her hands behind her back and then stepped back next to his partner.

Bethany looked the other man over. He was older, graying with a nice suit on. Lawyer or doctor, maybe? She couldn't be sure, but she didn't recognize him from anywhere. This guy must not have been someone they interviewed at any point involving the other murders. Maybe he was their leader, he was dressed better than any of the others. Well, except Dr. Montgomery but he was made of money.

She then checked out the office. There was a bench against the far wall with papers spread out over it. Bethany saw one of them was a map of the city. There was another metal chair behind the one she was sitting in, it had obviously seen better days. The entire office was covered in an inch of dust and dirt. She stopped looking around when she caught the new guy looking her over.

"Didn't your mother ever tell you, it isn't polite to stare?"

"You look just like him. You have his eyes." The well-dressed man stated."

"Like who?" Bethany questioned him.

The man walked closer to her, "I knew your father. We were partners."

"Partners in what?" Bethany's sassy tone fell away, her curiosity was getting the better of her.

"Well, now, you don't need all the details." The man grabbed the broken chair and sat in front of her. Surprisingly, it held him. "Let's talk about you."

Bethany leaned back in her chair. "I was told not to talk to strangers."

"Then let me introduce myself. You can call me Mr. Smith." The man smiled.

"Been to Washington lately, Mr. Smith?" She snarled.

Mr. Smith grew stern, "Now I'll be the one asking the questions. What do you know about us?"

Bethany smiled, "I know you're all murderers with bad manners. Not much else I need to know."

She could tell they knew just about as much as they did about what was going on. So apparently the lack of information was mutual between them. For them that was a good thing, for her that could mean a beating was in store to get what they needed. Bethany quickly looked around the room again for anything to help her escape or at least put up a good fight if that's what it came to.

"I heard a rumor lately," Mr. Smith started as he stood up, "that you could be considered a murderer as well."

"You shouldn't believe everything you hear." She spat, "Especially a rumor."

Mr. Smith got in Bethany's face, "And you Ms. Andrews should watch your manners." He stood back, "I believe Junior over here has a mission to finish. Isn't that right Junior?"

Mr. Smith moved over to the bench to allow Junior to come to the front. Junior seemed to be waiting for approval before doing anything, which came in the form of a nod from Mr. Smith. Junior waited till Mr. Smith handed him something. Bethany couldn't see at first, but when Junior turned back around, she knew it was a gun.

"Yes Sir. I do, sir." Junior nodded.

"Well, isn't that cute. A master and his pet." Bethany had no patience for this. "Go ahead Junior, make your master proud." She quickly made her peace of maybe this being it for her. Bethany hoped if something were to happen to her that Baker would be able to finish the job.

Mr. Smith walked back over in front of their prisoner, "I'd be careful, this one doesn't listen very well." He glared at Junior before taking the gun back out of his hands.

Junior slunk back into the corner. "I'm sorry, sir."

"See, he's the last one to finish his job because he kind of allowed himself to get a crush on his target." Mr. Smith explained.

"Well, I appreciated the notes and flowers." Bethany sarcastically stated, "They were everything a girl could have ever wanted."

Bethany caught Junior perk up at her statement. He apparently didn't know what sarcasm was. Mr. Smith once again glared at Junior and Bethany saw just how whipped the man was. This Mr. Smith figure definitely had a hold over Junior and it appeared as though violence of some sort may have played a role.

"As I was saying." Mr. Smith continued as he sat back down. "You are the last on the list, and thankfully we have a few more hours before that list needs to be completed."

"Do you all turn into pumpkins if it isn't finished in that time?" Bethany asked.

Mr. Smith waved the gun motioning Junior over to the bench, "Get her some duct tape would you. She doesn't need to talk, she just needs to hear what I have to tell her."

Junior grabbed the duct tape from the bench and pulled off a piece, carefully putting it over Bethany's mouth. She had lost her opportunity to ask questions and knew she didn't have much leverage this way. Mr. Smith once again grabbed the chair and sat down in front of her. He got comfortable as best he could before leaning forward.

"If tonight doesn't go perfectly, it will be your fault. You do need to die Bethany." Mr. Smith leaned back. "We have a few things to take care of first and then we'll be back for you. It'll be much more meaningful if you are sacrificing tonight." Mr. Smith stood, "Please make yourself comfortable while we're gone."

Mr. Smith motioned for Junior to follow him. Together they left the office. Bethany could hear them mumbling something as they went down the stairs. She watched as they walked through the factory out of her sight.

Taking the opportunity that was at hand, Bethany tried to escape her bondage. The rope was too tight, but maybe if she tried to move the chair over to the wall she could reach her phone. She tried to hold onto the chair back and try to scoot the chair over. With a loud thud the chair fell to the side and Bethany found herself on the ground. She laughed to herself. Definitely didn't go as smoothly as she was hoping.

She could hear footsteps running her way. Bethany sighed, the sound of her falling probably alerted Mr. Smith of her trying to escape. Oh great, they'd be back over here any minute. The footsteps got louder. There were definitely more than two people heading her way though. Something wasn't right.

"Sir, I got her over here." A male voice shouted.

"Well, look what we've got tied up." Another voice stated while kneeling beside Bethany.

Bethany looked up and smiled, "It's about time you boys found me."

"You're an idiot." Baker mentioned while he helped right the chair. "Now hold still so I don't cut your hand off." Baker cut the rope holding Andrews and helped her stand. "What were you trying to accomplish here?"

"Well, I met the leader of this stupid cult." Andrews mentioned while pulling the ropes off her wrists. "He called himself Mr. Smith."

"We got a lead to check this place out from the community center." Baker motioned out into the factory, "brought a few other officers with us to scout the place."

Andrews nodded, "Understood. So I'll be on my way then."

Baker grabbed her arm, "I can't let you go again, and you may end up dead next time."

"Noah. Not when I got you for my knight in shining armor." Andrews said pulling herself free. "Thanks again partner!"

Bethany took off down the stairs and snuck around the back of the factory. She took off through the parking lot and down one of the alleys. Going back to Julia's car would be a mistake, she'd have to find another means of transportation. First, though, she needed to rethink her methods. She needed to think up where should could find information on this Mr. Smith guy. Bethany crouched behind a bush to hide from the officers searching the parking lot.

Eventually the cops cleared out. Bethany had hoped Mr. Smith and Junior hadn't seen the commotion and would return. The cops probably took everything they found with them, but maybe there was something they missed. It was worth a shot anyway. Bethany needed a starting point to find Junior at the very least.

She snuck back into the factory and up into the office. Her instincts were right they had taken everything that had been there. Bethany knelt down to check under the desk, maybe they dropped something. In the distance she could hear a door bang close. The cops must have forgotten something. Bethany crawled her way back over to the steps and down around the corner. She found a safe place to hide, hoping this time she didn't get caught.

The voices grew louder as the people approached. It wasn't the cops, it was Junior and Dr. Montgomery. They were discussing something that was supposed to happen tonight. As they got closer, Bethany could make out more of the details.

"We really need to find Miss Andrews for you before tonight." Karl mentioned to Junior as they approached the stairs.

Junior nodded, "I know. Master won't be pleased if I haven't finished my mission."

"Pleased? He won't let you meet him if you don't finish your mission." Karl replied.

Bethany tilted her head in confusion. How could Junior not get to meet the master? He was with their leader when she was here before. Mr. Smith was the leader. She held her head, bracing herself for it to sink in. Mr. Smith couldn't be the leader, he was just another pawn. The puppet master was still out there and completely unknown to the police.

"Weren't you scared when you did it though?" Junior asked Karl.

"I wasn't the idiot that picked a cop as my target," Karl told him, "That was stupid on your part."

Junior nodded, "I know, but she's as close to her dad as I could get."

"Well then you're the one that's going to have to try and deal with that." Karl brought up.

"She's just a woman, can't be that difficult." Junior stated starting up the steps. "Hey, why don't you go get the box from the back while I collect all this stuff and take care of my task?"

"Sounds good," Karl replied before turning around and walking back.

The moment came when Bethany saw her chance to make a move. Junior had gone up to the office alone and Karl seemed to be leaving once more. Bethany followed him for a while to the front of the factory, making sure to stay out of sight. When she saw an opportunity to take him out down, out of sight of Junior, she moved in closer. Bethany snuck up behind Karl and put him in a headlock, letting him fall to the ground unconscious. She grabbed his ankles and pulled him behind one of the machines. Searching his passed out body, she found he was carrying a gun on him. Bethany checked the chamber and clip and found it was loaded.

Moving back toward the office, Bethany made sure to stay hidden again. She could see Junior moving around the office frustrated that nothing was where he left it. He also kept kicking the chair still over on its side. He was scratching his head when Bethany walked up the stairs holding her gun out. She got directly behind Junior and cocked the gun.

"Did you miss me?" Bethany sneered.

Junior turned around to face her. He raised his hands and fear flashed across his face. "I see you can't get enough of me." Junior started circling, "You managed to get loose, apparently and yet you stuck around to continue this party."

"Well, you know me, I'm just a woman. Can't get enough parties."

Junior smirked, "Let's keep chatting to give my friend time to come join us. There is always more fun than two."

It was Bethany's turn to have the edge, "Oh, you mean Dr. Montgomery," she paused, "yeah he won't be joining us anytime soon. I already said my hellos."

Junior seemed surprised, "You're going to ruin everything. Why can't you just let me kill you?"

"I will shoot you if necessary, but I would like some answers first." Bethany knew she was being hopeful that Junior would tell her anything. Plus, she had to make this quick before Karl woke up and she was outnumbered again.

Junior lowered his hands, "What would you like to know?"

Still holding the gun out, pointed directly at Junior's face, Bethany asked, "What part did my father have in all this?"

"Your father was this. Mr. Smith took your father's place." Junior has a smile on his face as he told Bethany about her father. He could tell it was upsetting her. "Your father was an amazing apprentice," he paused, "till he had you."

"What do you mean?" Bethany asked. She was trying to hold it together and not get emotional. She needed to know the truth.

Junior stepped closer, "He decided to go straight when he had you. He screwed us all over and tried to leave. No one leaves the group, so he was killed."

Bethany slowly started dropping her gun while processing the information. Junior took the chance to knock it from her hands and charge her. She got a punch in before pushing him off of her. They fought for a while, but it was clear Bethany could overpower him and with her anger, she was a force. Junior didn't give up. They both continued to fight, causing blood to splatter over the office. Eventually Bethany got control of the situation and pushed Junior down into the chair. She picked up the gun from the floor and aimed it back at his face.

"Enough!" She screamed.

By now Karl had come to, a little dizzy and with a massive headache but able to stand. He had heard all the commotion and was making his way to the back to the office. As he neared the office, he could see Bethany had Junior at gun point. They were arguing about something. He then watched as Junior slumped in the car and fell to the ground. The gun shot rang out through the factory. Karl hid behind a piece of equipment and watched as Bethany searched Junior and grabbed his extra clips. She hurried down the stairs and back around the office, disappearing through the back of the factory.

Karl slowly walked up to the office where he had just watched Junior get shot. He bent down next to him and checked for a pulse. Feeling a heartbeat, Karl leaned back to find the entrance wound. He located it on Junior's shoulder and put pressure on it. Junior wasn't dead, but he would be shorter if the bleeding didn't stop.

"Hello, Dr. Montgomery." Bethany whispered into his ear.

Karl stood up and backed away from Junior. "You didn't kill him?"

"Sadly, no, I'm not a murderer, but I did shoot him so he'd shut up." Bethany waved the gun, directing Dr. Montgomery to take Junior's place on the chair.

"Going to shoot me too?"

"First, I have a question. Where are the rest of your little friends meeting up later, so the master can thank you for his dirty work?" She questioned the man.

Karl nodded, "I see what you're after. It'll never work. The master has been already 10 steps ahead of you, he cannot be stopped."

Bethany was growing tired of the games. She pointed the gun at Karl's shoulder and fired. Unlike Junior he didn't pass out and just glared at her. "Whoops, did I do that? Guess my finger slipped."

"You bitch! You will die. You're weak, like your father!" He hissed, "He found you and has been watching you. No one survives when the master wants them dead."

She moved over and kicked Karl in the face, causing him to become unconscious. "Oh, shut up."

Bethany took her leave. As she walked out of the factory she called 911 to report hearing gun shots on the property and then took off into the night. Not knowing where to go next, she found refuge in an alley. Catching her breath, she decided to check in with Baker and see how it was going.

He picked up immediately, "This is Baker."

"Hey, I left you a present at the factory you guys were just at." She rubbed her neck, "I have no more leads, and do you have anything?"

Baker sighed over the phone, "We're following up on the other names we have, and I'll let you know when we have more."

"Sounds good. I did find out though that apparently my father had a lot to do with what was going on." Andrews could hear Baker sigh, "Can you look into him for me. Sounds like he was the first Mr. Smith before this group killed him."

"How do you know they killed him? They got the guy in jail already." Baker responded.

Andrews was realizing just how confused, she was about all this, "I know. Junior told me they called my father because he wanted out of their boys club. Please just look into it and then get back to me with whatever they find."

"Will do. Oh, and someone wants to talk to you." Baker said.

Bethany could hear him passing off the phone and then her heart dropped when she heard the voice on the other end, "Kevin."

"Bee where are you? I'll come get you. You don't have to run alone." Kevin anxiously told her.

"No. I need to do this alone. They know about my dad Kevin, I need answers." Bethany knew she had to hang up before she lost her edge. "I have to go."

"I lost you once, I can't lose you again. Please tell me where you are," he pleaded.

"Bye Kevin." Bethany said before hanging up the phone.

Now she was just one big girly mess of emotions. She hated how he could do that to her. Bethany decided to go for a quick run to get her head back in the game and try to think about where to go next. There had to be something Junior or Dr. Montgomery had said to give her a clue as to where this was all going down tonight. Bethany took off running down the alley.

Chapter 14: Bandlings

Andrews was enjoying a quick bite to eat when her phone rang. She picked it up, "Hey Baker. Find something already?"

"Yeah, we found something all right." Baker said angrily "What did we say about shooting people?"

"It was in self-defense. Can you blame a girl?" Andrews replied.

Baker sighed deep, "I can't keep protecting you and standing up for you if you continue to shoot people."

"I know, but you have them in custody now so what's the big deal?"

"Big deal, Andrews is you're not thinking like a cop. You're getting emotional. Now back off the case and let us handle something. Just lay low and relax." Baker demanded of her.

Andrews was inpatient, "Can you just let me know when you find something please and enjoy your little present."

"Last time, though Andrews. Don't let me catch you shooting anyone else!" Baker scolded before hanging up the phone.

Ok, so maybe Baker was right and she was a little out of control. Granted, she just found out that her father was involved with some sort of murderous cult and that Junior had tagged her as his target because of her father. Andrews hated what she knew she had to do next, but it was her next lead. She jimmied herself into a car parked nearby and started driving.

Bethany parked the car a few miles away and started on foot. It didn't take her long to get back to the house, she felt like she had just spent time on. She reached the back door and knocked after finding it was locked. The door opened and Bailey ran out to greet her.

"Hey girl, I missed you too." Bethany directed at Bailey, petting her behind the ears.

Loretta opened the door farther, letting Bethany in the house. "To what do I owe the pleasure?"

"We need to talk." Bethany stated walking past Loretta into the living room.

Loretta sat down, "What do you want to discuss?"

"I recently found out that dad was involved with the case I'm working on. Do you know anything?" Bethany questioned.

"I knew he was into some really bad stuff, but I thought he had given that up when he met your mother." Loretta added.

Bethany shook her head, "Apparently he tried but they frown on people leaving their little club and had my father killed."

"That's in the past, your father was a good man when you were born. He cared a lot for you and your mother." Loretta continued, "Don't hold his mistakes against him."

"I need to find out just what exactly they were first. I'm still working on figuring out his connection in all of this and thought you might be able to help me." Andrews pulled out her phone, "Do you recognize any of these men?"

Andrews had snapped some pictures of Junior and Karl while hiding in the factory. She watched the Loretta's face as she thumbed through the pictures. There was never a hint of recognition, so she must not have known them. Loretta handed back the phone and shook her head no.

"It was worth a try. They apparently were really close to my dad and knew him well when he was working for their so called master." Bethany put her phone back in her pocket. "I guess I don't have the leads I thought I did."

"Sounds like maybe you need to clear your head for a bit. Why don't you go and rest, look at it fresh in a few hours." Loretta suggested. "I'll wake you if anything comes up."

Bethany went to lay down for a little, Bailey following close at her heels. She laid there for a while looking up at the ceiling, thinking about the case and what she found out about her father. Pulling her phone out of her pocket, Bethany dialed a number and then waited. She listened to the phone ring on the other line till a man picked up.

"Uncle Pete?" Andrews asked.

Pete Mitchell wasn't surprised to be hearing from his niece, "What happened to laying low for a while?"

"A while turned into forever." Andrews stated, "I need you to fill in the blanks about my father."

"There isn't much I know about him. He was only around a few years after you were born and then he disappeared." He paused, "then a buddy showed up and he was murdered."

"Did he seem worried about something though? Was there anything that seemed off?" Bethany questioned.

Chief Mitchell yawned, "Honey, it's getting late. I don't really know anything more about your dad. He was a man of mystery, there weren't many people who knew much about him."

"Alright. Do you think mom would know anything?"

"No. Don't call your mom. She's upset as it is, considering your face has been in the news a lot lately for an accessory to murder." Pete added.

"Lovely." Bethany did not plan on being wanted for murder. She didn't put the gun in Carson's wife's hand.

"Stay low Bethany and let the cops do their job." Pete ordered.

"I am a cop. I was the cop. This is my case, I'm not going to just sit around and wait." Bethany grew upset.

"Fine, then just stay safe and out of sight. Call me if you need anything else." Pete then ended the conversation, "Goodnight Bee."

"Night, Uncle Pete."

Bethany put the phone down, and rolled over on her side. She watched Bailey's breathing and how calm the lab was, sleeping on her bed. Bethany finally started to relax and fell into a deep sleep. Her body was exhausted and needed some rest desperately, it had been a crazy few days.

"Daddy!" A little girl squealed with delight.

A man in a suit held out his hands, enveloping his daughter in his arms. "Hello my little bumble bee. I missed you."

The girl leaned back and put her hand on the man's cheek. "You get to stay now?"

"Only for a moment, my love." The man put his hand over his daughter's.

"When do you have to leave?" She started to tear up, "I don't want you to go." The little girl wrapped her arms around her father's neck. "Please don't leave me."

He stroked her hair for a while, "You'll be okay. While I'm gone you take care of your mother. Can you do that for me?"

"Yes" She whimpered quietly. The girl had a feeling she may not see her father again. "When will you be back?"

"Daddy needs to go see Mr. Smith for a little." The man stood up and kissed his daughter on the forehead before giving her one last hug goodbye, "I love you to the moon and back my little bumble bee."

"I love you to the star daddy." The girl clung to her father as long as she could before he peeled her off and walked away. The girl started to cry and fell to the ground, wishing her father would come back.

Bethany woke suddenly and sat up straight. She knew what she had dreamed was really a memory of the last time she saw her father. He had mentioned Mr. Smith that day before he left. That collaborated Junior says her father had been a part of their group. She wondered if her father had known he wouldn't be returning, that he was walking to his death.

The phone ringing shook Bethany from her thoughts. She checked the caller ID, it was Baker. "Yeah, do you have something for me?" she asked.

"Andrews, I need you to come down to the station." Baker stated. "You've been cleared of all charges, but we need your help on this case."

Odd timing, she thought, "How do I know you're telling the truth and not just baiting me?"

"Andrews, I wouldn't lie about this. You're my partner, I need you to come down to the station and help us." He stated.

"Alright, I'm not too far I'll be right there." Andrews hung up the phone.

She stood and went back out to the living room where Loretta was watching TV. She grabbed her keys, ignoring her grandmother's questions and walked out the door. Jogging the few miles back to the car she stole, she got in and started for the station. As she neared, nothing looked out of place or suspicious, so she pulled into a parking spot. Bethany got out of the car, looking around and ready to run if that became necessary. Slowly, she walked up to the door of the station. Once she realized no one was waiting for her, she walked in.

The receptionist didn't look up so Andrews continued walking to the Baker's desk. He was sitting there working on something. Baker looked up and waved Andrews over. She walked over to his desk and sat across from him.

"Seriously, there's no one here to arrest me?" Andrews asked looking around.

Baker laughed, "No, now stop being paranoid. Captain was thankful for your present so he dropped the warrant for your arrest and said you could come back to help."

As if the captain knew he was being talked about, he came over to where Baker and Andrews were. "Andrews my office now."

"Right behind you sir." Andrews said, rolling her eyes so Baker could see before following the captain.

Andrews followed him into the office and sat down in one of the chairs. The captain sat down and just looked Andrews over. The two exchanged glances for a while and Andrews thought the captain seemed to be waiting for something.

"You're a piece of work Andrews. Your uncle and I can't agree on what to do with you." Captain Harris stated, "He wants you locked up in jail, and I want to ship you out of my department."

"And what did you two decide on them?" Andrews asked.

"Why don't you try explaining your actions first and we'll see how forgiving I am." Harris leaned back and folded his hands waiting for her story.

"Fine. I was kidnapped, escaped somehow, went looking for my kidnappers and realized I had become a wanted felon for some reason. I had nothing to do with Carson's death, his wife killed him, not me." Andrews' voice was rising, "And then I got kidnapped again, escaped and thought you two wanted murderers. Oh, and I found out that my father was somehow involved in this mess."

"We received your gift," He paused, "A little more bloody than we would have liked."

Andrews smiled, "They tried to escape."

"I'm sure they did." Captain Harris leaned forward, "Now what does your father have to do with this?"

"He apparently was part of the group before I was born. He tried to leave and messed something up so they killed him. Junior tagged me as his target because whatever my dad did affect Junior." Andrews paused, "Wait, Junior is younger than me, but he was talking like he knew my dad and that's why he was targeting me. He said my dad screwed everything up for him."

"Junior couldn't have known your dad though, if he died while you were young." Captain Harris.

"Exactly." Andrews had more questions than answers at this point. "Do you have anything on Mr. Smith or who the master is?"

"Let me get Baker in here." Captain Harris dialed for Baker to report to his office. "Before he gets here, if you ever go rogue like that again, I will have your badge. Do you understand detective?"

"Yes, sir." Andrews answered.

They waited for Baker to get there. It was only a moment before he walked in with a stack of files and papers. He handed them to Andrews before sitting down. She quickly flipped through the files looking at everyone they had pegged as being involved in this.

"We have most of those involved and that have already killed their marks. We're still looking for Mr. Smith and the master." Baker filled Andrews in.

Captain Harris turned to Baker, "Have you ever found any connection between her father and this group?"

"No, there hasn't been a mention of any Andrews." Baker answered.

Andrews thought for a moment, "No, it would have been Mr. White. Dad referred to himself as Mr. White when he would Skype with his partners."

Baker took one of the files he had handed to Andrews, "That name I have come across. A few of those we picked up today had mentioned a Mr. Smith and a Mr. White." He paged through the file, "Here it is, they mentioned them trying to become the master."

"My father is dead, he can't become the master. They must be talking about someone else." Andrews added in.

"Ok, so we're after Mr. Smith and Mr. White. Those should be the only ones left," Andrews paused, "if they're replacing the master, then the master isn't alive anymore? Or can the master retire?"

"I don't know, do people retire from being serial killers?" Baker brought up.

Andrews turned to Baker, "Probably not. Did any of the others give you a tip as to where to start looking?"

"Yeah, we've already sent officers to all those locations to look. Each of them came up empty." Baker noted.

Andrews tried to think, "I have an idea of where to look."

"Please fill us in detective, where would we look?" Captain Harris asked.

"My grandmother lives near here, I've been staying with her. My dad grew up in Buffalo, and one of the plays he would always talk about and forbid me from going was the old post office downtown." Andrews couldn't believe she never thought of this before. "It was abandoned so of course, as kids we wanted to go exploring, he always yelled at me for it."

"It's worth a shot" Baker said as he stood up. "Care to ride along?"

Andrews turned to the captain for approval. "Go ahead, but try not to shoot anyone." Harris ordered.

Baker and Andrews left and got into the squad car. Andrews pointed over to the car she had driven here, "I stole that. It needs to be returned to the right owner. And where's Kevin?"

"I sent him back to your apartment to rest. Perez is watching over him." Baker told her. "How are you holding up?"

"I'm okay." Andrews told him. "I just want this over."

They rode the rest of the way in silence. Baker pulled over a block away from the post office. There were no cars out front, but it didn't look as abandoned as she remembered. They got their guns and slowly made their way to the building. Signaling to each other, Andrews tried the door handle and found it was unlocked. She slowly opened the door and let Baker go in first.

Guns still out, they moved behind the desk and checked the back rooms, one by one. All of the rooms were empty. It was obvious someone had been there recently. They heard a noise behind them and turned to see Mr. Smith is trying to escape out the front. The detectives took off after him, finally getting him cornered in an alley.

"Mr. Smith, you are suspected of running a hit ring." Baker turned the man around and put handcuffs on him.

Andrews reads Mr. Smith his rights and assisted her partner in getting the suspect in their squad car. The man sat in the back of the car quietly with a smirk on his face. Baker drove to the station, helping the man out of the car and into the building. They took him into one of the interrogation rooms, making sure to take him past the rest of his crew. Each person's expression fell once they saw Mr. Smith had also been caught. Their game was up.

Chapter 15: Rainworm

Mr. Smith was put into the chair facing the two way mirror and handcuffed to the table. Andrews and Baker took their seats across from him. Baker grabbed the folder and took the victims' pictures from the file and laid them out in front of Mr. Smith. His expression never wavered, which led the detectives to silently agree on a new approach.

"We already have you for kidnapping, assault against a police officer, evading the police, trespassing, and conspiracy to commit a murder." Andrews listed and then added, "Am I missing anything?"

Baker also spoke up, "We have the rest of your group singing like canaries already so there's no need to act tough."

Mr. Smith finally dropped the smirk, "You have no actual evidence that I am involved in any of this, or I would be in a cell already." He paused for a moment, "I would like to speak to my lawyer."

"You don't get to lawyer up." Andrews grew angry, "You don't get off that easy. Are there any other victims that we don't know about?"

Their suspect just sat there quietly, his smirk had returned. Slowly his eyes went to the pictures on the table. Making sure not to change his expression he looked them over, pleased with himself. Even with tonight's plans being put on hold, he knew things would continue without them. Mr. White could finish the ceremony.

Andrews and Baker eventually gave up on getting Mr. Smith to talk without a lawyer. The left him in the interrogation room and headed down to the lab to check on his finger prints and figure out who he really was. They got downstairs and went over to Sally Reynolds the fingerprint technician at the department. She was a perky recent college graduate who was always really excited about taking suspect's fingerprints and running them in the system.

"Hey Sally, did you get a hit yet on Mr. Smith?" Baker asked the girl.

"Sure did Detective. His real name is Joseph McKinley." Sally handed over the results and went back to work on another set that had come in.

Andrews recognized the name and it took her a moment to realize where it was from. "That's an old college friend of my dad's."

"Really?" Baker questioned his partner. "You're sure?"

"Yeah, I remember him bringing up that name when he would tell me stories." Andrews' heart sunk that would mean her father probably was involved in this cult before he died. "Let's go see if we can talk to Mr. Smith again."

Baker nodded, "It looks like he's wanted in a few states for different crimes. If nothing else, we have him on that."

"I want him for this." Andrews said through gritted teeth, "Those victims deserve their justice."

"He lawyered up Andrews, there isn't much we can do till his lawyer gets here." Baker knew that wouldn't be enough but they had to wait.

"I don't care, I need to talk to him." Andrews headed for the interrogation room.

Mr. Smith was still alone in the room, his lawyer must not have gotten there yet. She entered the room and put the fingerprint results in front of him. He looked at the paper and then back up at Andrews. Mr. Smith sat there silently, waiting for the detective to start.

"Joseph McKinley." Detective Andrews stated. "We found out that you are not Mr. Smith as you would have liked us to believe."

"Should I congratulate you Detective?" Mr. McKinley answered.

Andrews smiled, "I should remind you that you requested your attorney present."

"I remember, but it looks like you have something to ask me." Joseph probed, "Something bothering you."

"Do you know my father?"

"I believe you already know the answer to that." He replied.

Andrews could feel her heart starting to beat faster, "Then tell me how he was involved in all this!"

"You need to talk to Mr. White." McKinley told her.

The door to the interrogation room opened and a well-dressed man with a briefcase walked in. "Mr. McKinley say nothing more." The man turned to Andrews, "I'm his attorney and if you have nothing to charge him for, we will be on our way."

"Actually," a voice from behind the man started, "we have him on a few charges so he can't leave." Baker had joined the others in the room.

"I would like a moment with my client then." Joseph's attorney brought up.

The two detectives left the room. They waited outside the door for about twenty minutes before the attorney came out requesting to talk to the captain. After the captain went in and talked with Mr. McKinley and his attorney he came out with a somber look.

"We need to talk, follow me." Captain Harris led them both to his office.

He sat them down and explained how Joseph had taken a plea deal for his past crimes by giving information on the rest of the murder cult. The captain watched Andrews stand up and start to pace. He went on to explain that McKinley was going to get a reduced sentence of five years in jail, with a possibility of parole. The rest of them were going away for life since they now had enough evidence to place them at each murder.

Andrews had to sit back down, the blood had rushed from her face. "That's it? Five years?"

"I'm sorry detective, he gave us a lot of good information and all his past offenses are misdemeanors." The captain then continued, "Now I know you were looking into your father's case."

"Yes sir" Andrews shook her head.

"Since this case is now closed, I will have someone go to the archives and pull everything we have on his murder. If you happen to connect Mr. McKinley to your father's murder, we will revisit his sentencing." The captain excused the two detectives from his office.

Baker knew his partner wasn't satisfied with the outcome but sometimes that's how it went. "You going to be okay?"

"No. And what about Mr. White? He's still out there and could be killing." Andrews stated.

"There's no evidence of a Mr. White actually existing. Once the rest of them found out Mr. Smith had talked, they all confessed to their respective murders and your kidnapping." Baker paused, "It's over Andrews, and you're going to have to accept that."

"It's not over. Not for me."

Baker gave her a questioning look. "Does that mean you're going to be hanging around her then for a while before going back to your old department?"

"I'm not going anywhere till I figure out what happened to my father and I catch Mr. White." Andrews turned to walk away. "Even if it means I need to hunt him down by myself, I will find him."

Baker watched his partner as she walked away. He saw a change in her from when she first arrived but these past few months had been hell for both of them. Retirement was fast approaching and looking better and better every day. He promised himself to keep an eye out for Andrews but after this case, he knew he wouldn't be able to keep up with her anymore. He wasn't sure what she was going to do next, but he knew she would want to do it alone. Plus, he had a girl he had to walk down the isles in a few days, so this case needed to be far behind him.

Epilogue: Fleshflies

A little south of Buffalo, in Pittsburgh was a cottage that sat back into the woods. The cottage was quaint and it had little windmills that stood by the front door. It was well shaded by trees, passing vehicles could not see as they drove by. Residing in this cottage was a couple who had long hated each other, but could not possibly leave one another. Rarely seen together in society, they stayed secluded in their cottage hidden away.

Alone in their home, they never had any visitors and so it was unusual the one morning when a stranger came to visit. The man stopped by the mailbox at the end driveway, pausing to run his fingers over the Yoder name that was etched into the side. He continued his way up the driveway smelling the air and smiling to himself as he looked around reminiscing. The man made his way to the door, waiting and listening to the noises within the home. Finally, he reached up and knocked on the door anxiously.

"Randy get the door, I hear someone knocking." A woman about forty yelled from the kitchen.

Shuffling to the door, a man in his late forties grumbled under his breath, "Yes, you hag."

Randy opened the door, peering to each side looking for someone who could have been there, stepping out the door he scratched his head confused. He walked back inside, shutting the door behind him and taking a seat on the couch.

"You're hearing things old woman, there's no one out there." Randy picked up the remote and turned on the TV. He held his finger over the volume button ready to tune out his wife.

The kitchen was silent. After a few minutes Randy knew something was wrong, his wife was never quiet. He got up and walked into the kitchen.

"Betty dear, are you in here?" Randy saw no one. The dishes were still piled, soapy water filled the sink. Lying on the kitchen table was a note with a lyric scrawled on it. He went over to pick it up and read it aloud, his hand shaking as he held the paper.

248

"I knew an old lady who swallowed a fly... perhaps she'll die."